Llantó de la mujer

WOMAN'S cry

A NOVEL BY
VANESSA MÁRTIR

This is a work of fiction. names, characters, places, and incidents are products of the author's imagination or are used fictitiously and are not to be construed as real. Any resemblance to actual events, locales or organizations, or persons, living or dead is entirely coincidental.

Copyright 2007 by Vanessa Martir
ISBN: 0975945386

Edited by Lisette Matos
Design/Photogaphy: Jason Claiborne

All rights reserved. No parts of this book may be used or reproduced in any manner whatsoever without written permission, except in the case of brief quotations embodied in critical articles and reviews. For further information contact Augustus Publishing

First printing Augustus Publishing paperback May 2007

AugustusPublishing.com
info@augustuspublishng.com

A C K N O W L E D G E M E N T S

I owe so many thanks to countless souls ... The Divine for bestowing me with a gift that I've often felt unworthy of. I now see that my sometimes turbulent existence was in preparation for something greater, fodder for my writing, for the countless stories I have to tell.

To my daughter, for being the vital water and sunlight that this seed needed to flourish. Vasialys, you are the most profound and exquisitely painful love I've ever experienced. You bring joy to my every day. You are my greatest Muse. Everything I do is for you and because of you darling. Mommy loves you to pieces.

To my Mom and second Mom Millie for instilling in me a thirst for knowledge and a solid belief in my abilities. You've both made me strive for more, never deeming any endeavor impossible or unreachable. Millie, your loss has left a hole in my world that will remain for an eternity. Still, I hear your voice in my dreams coaxing me along, never letting me give up. Thank you both for making me a better woman.

To my brother: You've always protected me and made me feel like there is nothing I can not accomplish. Thank you for your faith. Remember, no matter what happens you are forever my Superman.

To my sister for being the person I always sought to emulate. You made me work harder. It was you that made me realize my love for the written word. Thanks for being you.

To my all my family for supporting me and loving me. Titi, your strength and perseverance is admirable. Marielle, you are a young woman with so much energy and promise. Your inner beauty is astounding. Without my family, where would I be?

Tamiko, my best friend, sister from another mother, Godmother to my daughter. Jigga, you are my other half. I love you to death ma! Let's keep doing our thing! Pursuing our dream like a fiend convulses for his next hit. Always more, more, more, higher, higher, and higher!

To my boys at Augustus Publishing, Jay Clay and Ant; Jay, you always believed in me even when I didn't believe in myself. Gracias sunshine for keeping me on my toes! You will always be special to me. Ant, for continually reminding me of my gift and my need to share it with the world, although at times I didn't always agree with your methods, your belief in me is moving! Thank you both for helping me bring my dream to fruition. Time to blow up the literary world! Let's do this!

To all those who've crossed my path and helped shape the characters in this story and those to come, friends and foes alike, good lookin' out! And to the world, follow your heart's longing and the cosmos will pave the way for you. Believe it, manifest it! Hunt it, stalk it like a tiger does its prey! Then sink your teeth into it and let it nourish your soul. Blessed be!

1

I twirled the curl at the end of my braid as I stared blankly at the page before me. I'd read the same sentence at least ten times but couldn't manage to get into it. The text wasn't particularly difficult; it's just that my mind was elsewhere. I looked around the train station thinking that since I couldn't focus on my studies, I may as well people-watch. I noticed a young woman sitting on the other side of the bench. A backpack on her lap, she was engrossed by the book she was reading. So much so that she didn't even notice me staring at her. She was a young Latina like me, probably in her first or second year at Columbia University. I couldn't help but wonder what her life was like, where she was going. If only I were in her shoes and not in mine. If only I could go back to my first years at Columbia knowing what I now knew.

I was only two months shy of graduating from one of the most prestigious schools in the country and though this was supposed to be one of the happiest times of my life, I felt stuck and confused, like I was being pulled in opposing directions. A foreboding feeling of angst was wearing at me, not letting me concentrate. I had been living two lives for my entire college career and now more than ever I was feeling the effects. I was in love with a drug dealer and had spent five heart wrenching years trying to do right by him and living the street life while simultaneously going to school full time. I'd been through it with him, from him cheating on me left and right to him putting his hands on me and I'd forgiven him for it all, but now I was staring my future in the face and it didn't look as promising as it once did. I couldn't help but feel that everything was going to hit the fan soon and I didn't know how I was going to deal. I sighed deeply and stood up as the train roared into the station.

"Uptown #1 Train.. Next stop 125th Street," announced the conductor as the doors closed behind me.

I looked around and immediately spotted the cutie checking me out. I glanced at my reflection in the window and smirked. My long hair was parted down the middle, neatly braided Pocahontas style. I wore a white DKNY tank top and a low rise, fitted gray DKNY sweat suit with Classic K-Swiss sneakers. My flat mid section was exposed enough to reveal a pierced belly button and tight abs. I'm not conceited but I know I'm not ugly. Actually I'm quite attractive but never let that go to my head. I'm most proud of my intelligence and ability to survive and thrive despite the arduous circumstances that seem to constantly plague my existence.

"Would you like to sit down, Pocahontas?" asked the cutie. He was sitting in the seat next to the door I was leaning on.

I smiled shyly. "No, I'm okay, hun. I've been sitting for a while so I'm good for now but thanks for the offer."

"No problem. Just trying to be a gentleman," flirted the sweet looking Latino.

I glanced around and couldn't help but notice that he hadn't extended his "gentlemanliness" to any of the other females that were standing up. A couple of them shot hateful eyes at me but I opted to take my usual route and ignored them. I was used to being envied and learned long ago that the best thing to do was to disregard it altogether.

"Is that a book on Buddhism you're reading?" asked the lindo pointing at the book in my hands.

I eyed him curiously. I'd noticed his good looks immediately upon entering the train but as I peeped him now, I couldn't help but stare. He was even more handsome than I initially realized. His curly hair was cut into a short blow out. His beard was neatly trimmed and cut close to frame his jaw and he had a goatee that only complimented his full, kissable lips. Damn, I mused silently. If only I were single! I checked him out from head to toe. He wore a cream colored *guayabera* with dark jeans and what I could swear were Kenneth Cole shoes.

Mmmmm! Damn, I loved me some pretty boys but I'd never been unfaithful before despite what I'd been through with Fabian and I was not about to start now.

I glanced down at the book and observed that the cover was exposed. Buddha sat meditatively on a lotus flower. "Yeah, it's for a class I'm taking," I responded, blushing. I realized that I'd been sizing him up and my response was delayed long enough for him to notice. Shit! I was slipping in my game. I hadn't been in the game for so long that I hardly knew what I was doing anymore.

He smirked. "Let me guess, Indo-Tibetan Buddhism, right?"

I did a double take. Let me find out! What could he possibly know about that, I wondered.

"Shocked you didn't I?" he added quickly as if reading my mind. "I took a similar class when I was at NYU. So, you're a student at Columbia?" he asked.

I was taken aback. *¡Coño!* He's fine and he's learned. That's what I need in my life. I thought about my man and pursed my lips in frustration. "Yeah, I'm graduating in two months if all goes well."

"That's what's up. Beauty and brains! You're a full package, aren't you? So, I'm assuming you're off the market 'cause a female as fly as you couldn't possibly be single." His voice gave away a lingering hope that he was wrong.

"Yeah, you got that right," I said begrudgingly.

"Too bad. I would have loved to take you out to vibe intellectually." He didn't make the least attempt to hide his disappointment.

"Thanks, pa, but no thanks. I don't cheat. It's just not my style." I struggled to hide the hint of reluctance in my voice but knew I'd failed miserably. I hoped he didn't pick up on the bitterness but in the back of my mind I knew that these days it was written all over my face.

"Well, my name is Ruben. I hope we meet in the next lifetime. Stay beautiful and true," he said longingly as he got up. "This is my stop. I'll pray to Buddha that we'll meet again someday soon and hopefully, by then you would have shed yourself of those chains that bind you." He winked at me as he stepped off the train. "Wait, what's your name?" He held the door open with his foot.

"India." My face flushed with bashfulness. He nodded knowingly and we stared at one another mesmerized as the doors closed. Our eyes didn't break their gaze until the train pulled off.

See, that's what I need in my life, I thought to myself as I sat down in the still-warm seat that Ruben had been sitting in. A man with a future and intelligence, one that can stimulate me during the first few moments of an encounter is most definitely someone I'd like to get to know. If only I were single. If only my heart was open to that and not caught up in some drug dealer's grip. *¡Máldita sea!*

I glanced around the train again and saw that the haters were still glaring at me with nasty sneers on their lips. Two of them were blatantly bashing me, gossiping into one another's ears and cutting their eyes at me.

You wouldn't want to be in my shoes ladies. Hate me all you want but I'd trade places with you in a heartbeat if I could. I shook my head in disgust and pulled out my iPod. I'd decided to give up on reading. My mind just wasn't cooperating and it was obvious I wasn't going to get anything done in this state. I listened to some old-school freestyle while my mind wandered over the shambles that was my life.

2

"¡Perra!" a female voice yelled as I stepped off the train at Dyckman Street. I didn't have to look back to know that the slur was directed at me. I always wondered why chicks were always so spiteful towards one another. After all, wasn't there ample space in the sky for all the stars to shine? I had problems with females all my life. I couldn't count the times I'd thrown down and gotten jumped simply because of the confidence with which I carried myself. No matter how much effort I put into making myself approachable or how friendly I was, they tended to feel threatened by me and shunned me as a result. That was why all my life my closest confidantes had been male. I'd gotten over it but it still bothered me sometimes. Why should I shrink

myself to make others feel more secure around me? What the fuck is wrong with my sisters? I contemplated crossly. Whatever! Fuck them! I pushed my ponderings out of my head with a final thought, their hatred was their issue, not mine.

I turned my attention to the next issue at hand - my man. I wondered what mood he was in today. It was Friday, the beginning of the weekend, time to add up the tally for the week. If he'd made good money on his sales and the spot, he'd be in a good mood. It would be time to party, floss at the club and get fucked up on Moet and Grey Goose, and maybe even pop a couple of pills of ecstasy. If he hadn't made much money, he'd be irritable and would more than likely take it out on me. That's just the way he was.

I saw him standing in front of the pool hall talking to a group of girls that couldn't have been more than sixteen or seventeen. I could tell he was flirting; after all I'd spent the last five years of my life trying to win his heart. The sleeve of his Ralph Lauren Purple Label V-neck was unnecessarily rolled up, exposing his iced out Rolex. The sun sparkled off the two carat rock in his earlobe and the diamonds in the medallion of his thick chain. The girls were obviously enthralled by the display of money and Fabian's gift of gab. I was all too familiar with his ability to run game. I'd always thought that if he wanted to go legit, he'd probably have no problem being a car salesman because with his *muela,* he could easily sell a lemon to the most knowledgeable consumer.

Fabian nonchalantly pushed his Fendi shades up his nose,

shamelessly flaunting the Roli ring on his finger. He'd bought it to match the watch. It was all about the front, letting the world know that he had money. I quietly walked up behind him hoping to hear what he was saying to the girls.

"You know how I do ladies. C'mon, I'm the infamous, the one and only Fabian. Anytime y'all wanna hang, smoke an L, and chill, y'all just holler at me. Don't worry, I won't bite. I might nibble a little but never bite, unless of course you want me too." The girls giggled flirtatiously but silenced immediately when they saw me leering at them from behind Fabian, my head tilted to the side slightly, hand on my hip, daggers for eyes. They knew very well who I was.

"Fabian's wifey, yo," whispered one of them as if I couldn't hear. "Let's bounce."

Fabian turned around and grabbed me by the waist affectionately. "What's up, mami? I've been waiting for you. Where you been? Why didn't you call me? I would've picked you up."

"It sure doesn't look like it. Looks to me like you had your hands full," I responded accusingly, rolling my eyes and curling my lip with revulsion.

"Nah, baby. Just being nice to the custies. You know how it is ma. I gotta make money to spoil my queen, don't I? Their money buys you the world, boo. Give your pa a kiss."

"Yeah, whateva," I retorted but gave him a deep open mouth tongue kiss so everyone could see. I did it more for the group of little girls who were walking away but still glancing back longingly.

"You know you my moon, ma." Fabian grabbed my full, tight ass and pushed his crotch into mine.

"You're such a *sucio.*" I giggled and pushed him away half-heartedly.

"You hitting the gym hard, ma. That ass is on fire, baby," Fabian remarked, his eyes followed my jiggle as I walked into the store.

¡Que baina! I thought. No matter what he does, he still has that effect on me. Whenever I see him, my heart palpitates, palms become sweaty and I get a knot in my stomach.

I loved him and hated him at the same time. I'd been through so much with him, he'd broken my heart so many times and still I stood by him, taking his shit, hoping like a *pendeja* that one day soon he'd learn to love me like I yearned and deserved. At least he's in a good mood, I said silently to myself.

"C'mon baby," Fabian whispered into my ear as I peered into the glass refrigerator doors trying to figure out what flavor Gatorade to buy. "Let's go shopping. We gonna hit the town tonight and my mami gotta look fly. Whatever you want, price ain't an issue. Let's bounce." He reached over me to grab a Corona with one hand and groped my breast roughly with the other.

3

Sue's Rendezvous in Mount Vernon was the strip club to frequent if you were a drug dealer in the tri-state area. They gathered there to talk business, floss their money and ice, and, if they got lucky, take a dancer home for the night.

I gazed at the stripper's long thick legs as she worked the pole. This bitch is off the hook, I thought, staring at her gyrating, muscular ass. The stripper named Anais made it no secret that she was feeling me. She licked her lips and played with her nipples while staring coquettishly into my transfixed eyes.

Anais leaned over and whispered into my ear, "Love your Dolce dress, bella."

As she leaned back, she tenderly ran her finger down my

exposed cleavage. I shivered, the little hairs on my arms stood on end and my pussy became moist. I felt the E and Grey Goose coursing through my veins. The bass of the house music thumped to the rhythm of my heartbeat. I could feel Anais's touch down to my toes long after she had moved away to work the group of ballers sitting to my left. She glanced back every now and then to lock eyes with me and throw me a kiss to let me know she was coming for me. I sat there biting my lip in lustful anticipation, discreetly rubbing my hard nipples on the cold, dewy glass of vodka and cranberry in my hand.

I felt Fabian's hands move up my thigh. "You look devastating in that dress, ma. You see, your papí takes care of you."

I stared at myself in the mirror opposite me. The dress clung to my perky breasts exposing my lush cleavage and rippled midsection all the way down to my navel. It hugged my small waist and full hips stopping mid thigh to show off my well-developed thigh muscles. I wore strappy Manolo Blahnik stilettos on my French manicured feet. I felt like a diva in the dress and knew I shined. I turned heads the minute I stepped into the joint and relished in the attention, but as soon as Fabian saw that all eyes were on us, he gruffly grabbed my waist and led me around like I was his trophy. I felt like a prize dog on a leash at the Westminster Kennel Club show.

I grazed my fingertips up my defined arm and looked at my man. He wasn't the best looking man in the world with his thick as bottle bottom glasses and forty pound overweight frame but I loved him and loved the affection he lavished on me when he was mellow,

E'ed out and not wrapped up in his feelings. I smiled and kissed his lips. Despite his chubbiness, Fabian made sure he looked dapper wherever he went.

"You look so *lindo.*" I'd picked out his outfit; a black Gucci cotton silk blend mustique line pinstripe suit complimented by a white Gucci silk button up, diamond butterfly cufflinks and Gucci wingtips.

Fabian saw that I was admiring him and took advantage of the moment. "So that's the one, ma?" he asked innocently. "She the one we taking home tonight?"

I felt my body tense up momentarily, heat filling my chest cavity. My nostrils flared as I stared at him in disbelief but I quickly calmed myself down and let the soothing effects of the drugs take over. It's all good for tonight, I thought. I'm in the mood to feel the warmth of a woman's touch. I looked over at Anais who turned to simper seductively at me. I felt chills run down my neck to the small of my back as I watched the exotic dancer play with her clit through her flimsy g-string. Anais spread her legs and threw her head back in ecstasy, making my mouth and pussy water.

Fabian grabbed my chin roughly and turned my face to his. "What up, ma? It's like you like her more than you like me. What the fuck is up with that?"

I ran my fingers through Fabian's curls and let my index finger trickle down the back of his ear. I knew that drove him crazy and would calm him instantly. The last thing I needed was for this nigga to cause a scene.

"*Cójelo suave, papí.* It's for you, pa. All for you. I'm just working her to get her to come home with us. I got you, baby." I teasingly rubbed my hand on his hardening penis and softly traced his ample lips with the tip of my tongue.

Yeah right, I thought simultaneously. I want that bitch for me but if I have to do her while I do you, so be it. I couldn't have this nigga fuck it up for me.

I struggled with the ecstasy's tendency to make me emotional. For a moment I thought about the ménage trios we'd had in the past. My heart hurt and I had to blink repeatedly to fight the tears. I just couldn't believe the things I'd done to hold on to this man. He was not even close to being a GQ nigga and though he spoiled me with expensive gifts of clothing and jewels, what I really wanted he'd never given me - his heart and fidelity. Yet I'd done things for him and put up with shit that I'd always swore I never would for any man.

I can't think about that right now, I thought. If I get stuck on that shit, this E will fuck my head up and I'll be crying and moping for the rest of the night. *¡Que se jóda!* Fuck it! What's done is done, I scolded myself. I gulped down a shot of Hennessy and let the warmth fill my chest and alter my mood.

Just then Anais walked over with what looked like hundreds of dollar bills hanging from her G-string and spread out at her feet. I grabbed a wad of dollar bills out of Fabian's hand, looked at Anais and demanded mischievously, "Work for me baby." I stood up, winked at

Fabian, and began to shower Anais with dollars as the stripper danced for me.

It was obvious Anais had been doing this for a while. She was truly a professional. She took her time with every motion and every change of position. She bent down in front of me and swayed her body in rhythm to the music, mouthing the words to Amber's "Sexual" as she traced my torso with her fingertips.

> "Don't you know that when you touch me baby that it's torture/ Rub up against me, I get chills all down my spine/ When you talk to me, it's painful/ You don't know what you do to this heart of mine."

Anais left one hand delicately resting on my ass while her other hand roamed her own body. She began outlining the contours of her sharp-featured, stunning face, then moved down her slender neck to her ample breasts. She brought her nipple to her mouth and giggled as she licked and bit it, all the while watching me entranced.

I bit my lower lip hungrily as I watched her work me. It was like no one else was in the room but the two of us. The fact of the matter was that just about all the guys on our side of the club were fighting for a view of the lesbian show. A number of the guys began to throw five, ten and twenty dollar bills hoping to goad us to go even further in our performance. At that moment, Anais leaned over and lightly wiped the sweat off my brow. She then put her mouth to mine.

I closed my eyes and felt the heat of passion send shivers surging through my body. Our tongues wrapped around one another the way I imagined our bodies would later.

"Can I have some of that?" Fabian asked with a hint of jealousy in his voice. He rammed his face right in between ours, forcing the kiss to end prematurely, and grabbed my waist brusquely. I winced and stared at him with disgust but swiftly wiped the look from my face, giggling at him in an effort to hide my anxiety. I knew he'd make me regret the show I'd just put on. I hoped I could win him over and make him forget by giving him a threesome later on.

That's when I realized the ruckus that Anais and my display had caused. I saw bills thrown all over the stage – at least three times more than were there before we started. I laughed heartily and looked at Anais who was pointing at my feet. I looked down and all I could see were the bills on top of bills, so much so that I couldn't even see my sandals. The crowd didn't just tip Anais. They had thrown bills at me too.

"Encore, Encore!" they yelled as they grinned perversely at one another.

I looked at Fabian and saw the glint of jealousy in his eyes. I sat on his lap and kissed him. He bit my lip cruelly. "I told you this was for you, papí. *¡Suavé!*" I said apprehensively, wincing at the metallic taste of blood seeping from the fresh cut on my top lip.

"I'm sorry, mami," he responded half-heartedly. "It's the alcohol. You know Crystal makes me bruto. Did I hurt you, ma?"

He smoothed the back of his hand across my cheek bone repentantly. I knew better though. It wasn't the alcohol or the E. It was his possessiveness getting the best of him.

I'll make it up to him in a couple of hours, I thought. He'll forget all about this when Anais and I are sucking cum out his dick.

4

I leaned across and tousled Fabian's hair. He momentarily took his eyes off the road and smirked lustily at me. I looked towards the back seat of Fabian's 2005 Jaguar S-Type and met eyes with Anais.

"Wow, you're awe-inspiring in your beauty," I said aloud without realizing it. I felt Fabian's fierce look pierce me but chose to ignore it. He pressed his foot on the pedal, sending the shiny white Jag shooting up Gramaton Avenue. He could've gone 150 mph and we wouldn't have known any better. We were enthralled by one another and for the second time since we'd met hours earlier, we zoned out from the real world and entered our own little fantasy.

I mulled over Anais's crisp complexion. Her skin was a shade or two darker than the champagne leather seat she rested on. Her light brown hair cascaded down the left side of her face framing her chiseled cheekbones. Her lips looked enticing with their light coat of lip gloss. Her red silk halter dress hung loosely but I could just make out her hardening nipples. I licked my lips but before I could say a word, Anais leaned forward and put her index finger to my lips. Our lips touched, soft pecks at first, then deep open mouth kisses. Our eyes clung to one another all the while, barely blinking.

"Come sit back here with me bella," Anais said sweetly, running her fingers through my waist length hair.

I put my hand on Fabian's arm, feeling it tense as he gripped the wheel tightly. Without looking, I instructed him softly but firmly to pull over. Fabian reluctantly obliged and opened his mouth in silent protest and disbelief as I got out of the passenger seat and stepped quickly into the back. He adjusted his rear view mirror and gawked enviously as he watched Anais and I grope one another. His dick became rigid as he watched us devour one another.

Anais and I wasted no time with small talk. We allowed our passion to encase us like a cocoon. There were no words, no need for them; just hands and mouths against skin. Anais took over with deliberate ease. She subtly pushed me back and looked at me longingly up and down, chewing on her lip, as if to say "let me look at you." She moved my top to the side exposing both breasts, bowed slightly and licked my nipples in slow circular motions. She took her time. I knew she could feel me shudder as she trailed her fingertips along the small of my spine and suckled my nipple. I was in utter ecstasy and the E amplified the experience tenfold. I moaned as Anais entered a finger slowly into my pussy. She penetrated with shallow thrusts and stroked my g-spot ever so slightly before retreating torturously. I felt my insides throbbing with delight and purred when I felt my pussy explode then implode in orgasm. I giggled and opened my eyes only to be knocked abruptly out of my bliss. I met Fabian's stabbing gaze in the rear view and knew he was enraged. I smiled guiltily.

"Hold on, precious."

Anais retreated without question. I leaned forward and put my hand on Fabian's arm, kissed his face and whispered, "I didn't forget about you, baby. Don't worry."

His features softened and I felt his body relax as I rubbed his arm affectionately. Anais and I held one another during the remaining five minute ride to Fabian's condo on Tuckahoe Road. I stared at him in the rear view nervously, hoping to reassure him with my gaze. Fabian's wrath terrified me.

"I'm not feelin' your man, bella," Anais said as she affectionately pushed my hair behind my ear. Her other hand was around my waist. "This is about me and you beautiful." She kissed my neck.

"But..." I hesitated and pulled away. I looked back to see if Fabian had parked the car. "He's my man. He's gonna wanna get down. I thought you understood that."

"I don't want to cause any friction between you and your man, boo, but I have to be real. I'm just not diggin' him like that. His whole vibe bothers me. It's hateful and vicious. I came because I want you. I need to feel you." She drew me close. "I want to please you in a way you can't imagine. He can watch if he wants but that's it." She wrapped her tongue around mine and made me forget about Fabian. Neither of us saw him approach.

"Can I have some of that?" Fabian grabbed both our asses roughly. Anais cringed and tried to hide her repugnance but the quickness of her withdrawal gave it away. Fabian looked at her perplexed but before he could say anything, I planted a wet kiss on his open mouth.

"Wanna play, pa?" I asked, caressing his crotch.

We went upstairs together with me walking deliberately in between Fabian and Anais. When we entered the apartment, I lit candles, put Sade's Greatest Hits on the surround sound, and served us all tall glasses of Grey Goose and cranberry. I excused myself and went into the bathroom where I prepared a bath of jasmine essence and rose petals in the Jacuzzi.

I could feel the tension in the living room when I reentered. I heard Anais's pleasant raspy voice singing along to Sade's Smooth Operator and looked over to see Fabian rolling a huge L of 'dro. Anais and Fabian sat on opposite sides of the butter leather coach, not looking at or speaking to one another. We puffed the blunt while Sade's silky voice sang in the background.

When we finished puffing, I led them both to the bathroom. I pecked Anais and sat her down on the edge of the hot tub. "I'll be with you in a moment," I said with a flirtatious smile. Before I could turn around, I heard Fabian swiftly unzip his pants, rip off his shirt, popping buttons in his haste, and splash into the hot tub.

Damn, talk about thirsty! *¡Que lambón!* I thought unamused, arching my eyebrows at his annoying over-eagerness. I looked over at Anais. Her expression revealed that she was thinking the exact same thing.

Fabian looked at us both with a huge grin, shrugged and asked, "Y'all joining me or what?"

"Now you gotta wait for us," I responded.

Anais and I slowly began to undress one another in between kisses to the lips, neck and breasts. Fabian bit his bottom lip as he watched. We stepped into the tub. To Fabian's surprise, I placed myself in between him and Anais. I remembered what Anais had said to me and could tell from her body language that Anais was serious about not getting down with Fabian. I hurriedly kissed Fabian and jerked him off trying to distract him while with my other hand, I discreetly stimulated Anais's clitoris. Anais grabbed the loofah, poured some Victoria's Secret Forbidden Fantasy body wash on it and began to gently scrub my shoulders and back.

Fabian stood up and rammed his rock hard penis into my mouth. I gagged and tried to pull back but he grabbed me by the nape of my neck and wouldn't let go. My eyes watered but I let him manhandle me. I knew that if I tried to stop him, he'd go into a rampage and would kick Anais out or worse, get violent with us both. I sucked him off until he came, which wasn't long because despite his constant bragging, the truth was he was a three minute man.

Fabian clenched my hair, forcing me to keep his eight inches deep in my throat until the last drop of cum spewed from his dick. When he was done, he carelessly got out of the tub. "I'll wait for y'all in the bedroom," he muttered without even a glance back. I hadn't noticed that Anais had stopped bathing me and was staring open mouthed in shock.

"What the fuck was that?" Her voice held a mixture of anger and sadness.

"That was nothing, ma." I tried to hide the sorrow. "Now he'll leave us alone for a while."

Anais looked at me forlornly and cradled me in her arms. We bathed one another and kissed for what seemed like forever. By the time we went to the bedroom, Fabian had fallen asleep on the chaise longue opposite the California king size bed. We were both relieved but neither said anything.

We fell onto the silk sheets into each other's arms. Anais grabbed me by the wrists and held them over my head rendering me motionless. She bit me gently but firmly on the lips and neck.

"There's velvet rope in the top drawer," I whispered, coyly motioning towards the night table. Anais slipped the smooth cord around my wrists and in between the brass headboard, making it a point to leave them loose enough so she wouldn't have trouble changing my position. She then proceeded to slowly and methodically lick and nibble me from head to toe.

I whimpered as Anais worked her way down my torso. She

left no inch of my body untouched. When she reached my pussy, she licked my Brazilian waxed bikini line and stroked my clitoris but mischievously proceeded to kiss and bite around my crotch and on my inner thigh, not stopping until she reached the point of each toe. She then turned me around and did the same to my back.

I quivered and moaned uncontrollably when Anais reached the small of my back. This was one of my weak spots. I gasped in delight as she began to lick my ass and finger me from behind. Several times I felt like I was about to cum but just when I was about to reach the height, Anais withdrew and began to lick another spot and stimulate another area. I glanced at her, dizzy with rapture, and saw my juices dripping down her chin.

"Release me, please," I whispered desperately in between each pant of breath. "I wanna touch you, taste you. Let me go."

"No, bella," Anais tormented lovingly. "You're in trouble now." She flipped me over and began to eat my pussy in a way no one ever had, flitting my clitoris rapidly with her tongue while thrusting her middle finger into my pussy. I wriggled uncontrollably. All at once I wanted to pull away and push Anais further into my crotch. Anais tongued my clitoris and fingered me with increasing vigor until I squirted milky white cum. She licked it up and continued to enthusiastically stimulate my clit and g-spot while I shuddered wildly with orgasmic spasms. She made me cum another two times before finally relenting. She then ran her fingertips lightly over my torso and breasts while I, sweating and wheezing in excitement, caught my breath.

Anais pulled herself up towards my face. She loosened the rope while she kissed me intensely. I tried to mount her but she stopped me. "No, it's okay, bella. This wasn't about me. It was about you."

"But I want to please you," I pouted with disappointment.

"Oh you did. I came twice just watching you shake." She licked my lips. "You are exquisite, mami, and don't let anyone tell you otherwise."

We held one another, so caught up in the moment that neither noticed that Fabian had awoken and had been filming us.

6

I opened my eyes sleepily and squinted trying to force my eyes to adjust to the bright sunlight shining through the bay windows. I smiled, remembering the night, and extended my arm, expecting to feel Anais's soft skin. I groped the silk sheets but came up empty. I opened my eyes fully and looked around the room. Anais was nowhere to be found. Her clothes that had been lying on the red divan across the room were gone as well. I looked over at the chaise longue and saw that bare as well.

"Where is everyone?" I wondered.

I got up slowly and walked lazily to the bathroom. My pussy burned as I urinated; it felt like I had rug burn in my crotch.

"Ooooh," I winced loudly. "That bitch tore my pussy up," I

said laughing. "Put this ass to sleep."

I ran the shower and let the warm water cascade over my body. I touched my clit and shuddered, reminiscing about my encounter with Anais. Suddenly I felt a sharp pain in my side.

"Did you enjoy yourself, you fucking whore?!" asked Fabian furiously. He jabbed me in the ribs again and grabbed me by my hair. I struggled to break free. Before I could scream, Fabian punched me in the stomach and ribs, sending ripples of pain throughout my small frame and trapping my shriek in my throat. I collapsed into a heap. He pulled me to my knees by my hair and spat in my face. "What happened? I'm not good enough for you? I've never heard you scream like that when I fuck you? That bitch better than me? Huh? You fucking sucia!" He threw me down and spat at me again. He glowered at me pathetically as I balled myself into fetal position and sobbed quietly into my knees. "You fucking dyke!" he yelled as he threw a crumpled up sheet of paper at me. "Your lesbian lover left you a little note before she bounced. And she left you some money too, you fucking prostitute!" He threw the crumpled bills at me and stormed out.

I laid there rocking my bruised body. When I heard the front door slam, I leaned over and opened the wadded paper.

India,

You were amazing. I can't express how exquisitely you made me feel. I hope we can do this again. Next time, it must be just me and you. Give me a call mi bella. 646-555-4608.

Besos,

Anais

*P.S. I'm leaving this money because it's yours. You gave it to me at the club but that money was given to you by your admirers. Buy yourself something nice and be sure to wear it for me on our next encounter. *wink wink**

I counted the money and was amazed to find almost six hundred dollars. I recalled giving Anais the money and the look of hesitation on her face. I giggled and was quickly brought back to my excruciating reality by the sharp pain in my abdomen. I sobbed quietly, cradling myself, wondering what the fuck it was going to take to break the fuck out of this abusive relationship.

I lay on the hospital bed stunned. The nurse's words echoed in my ear.

"I'm sorry to have to tell you this but you've had a miscarriage, Ms. Maldonado."

Tears streamed down my face like rivers. "I was pregnant?" I asked in disbelief. "What do you mean?"

"Yes, you were about six weeks pregnant," the nurse replied sympathetically. "The good news is that we think you've discharged the entire fetus so we won't have to scrape your uterus."

I stared at her aghast. "I can't believe this shit!" I rubbed my belly and winced in pain. I was still badly bruised from the *golpeada* Fabian had inflicted upon me two days before.

The nurse walked to the door and closed it. She pulled up a chair alongside my bed and sat down with a look of concern. "I think those black and blues on your torso are what caused the miscarriage. You want to tell me what happened?" she asked, hopeful I would open up.

I tried to talk but choked up and began to sob uncontrollably. I remembered looking at my nude reflection in the mirror the night before. Ugly, green, black and blue contusions dotted my back and abdomen. I collapsed into the nurses' arms, heaving in dismay as I recalled the night of the beat down. I couldn't believe this had happened. It was surreal. Fabian had put his hands on me in the past but never so violently. The million dollar question was would he have been so sadistic had he known I was pregnant with his child. Despite my misery, I felt a sense of relief. I couldn't have a baby, not now, not with Fabian. My conviction surprised me.

I looked at the nurse. "Thank you but that's my past now. I'd rather not get into it." I wiped my nose with the bed sheet and grimaced at the overpowering smell of hospital, a mixture of disinfectant and medicine. "Thank you. I'm sorry." I gave the nurse my back and balled into fetal position.

"Well, if you want to talk, my name is Nurse Richards. You can call me Aimee. There's also a social worker on duty today. Her name is Ms. Lopez. Just buzz the call button and someone will come to help you. You can go whenever you like, no rush. Your clothes are in the bag at the foot of the bed. The doctor's specifications about post-ER care are on the table." The nurse hesitated. "I really wish you'd talk to someone about your injuries... Take care."

In the reflection of the glass on the closet door, I watched Nurse Richards look back at my shaking form. She shook her head disconcertedly and closed the door behind her.

I lay in the bed for a while mulling over the events of the past few days. I still couldn't believe that I had been pregnant. Tears rolled onto the bedspread as I thought about my deceased baby. I wondered if I would have actually gone through with the pregnancy had I not miscarried. Thoughts of my baby made me convulse with sadness. Maybe I should talk to somebody. Maybe talking to a counselor will help ease this pain, I thought.

The ring of my cell phone snatched me out of my thoughts. I knew it was Fabian by the ring tone – Changes by Mary J. Blige. He'd left five messages since I'd left his apartment without leaving so much as a goodbye note. I'd emptied my drawers and closet, taking even my razor, toothbrush and loofah. "Fuck that, I'm taking this shit," I'd thought contemplating the loofah. "I paid $15 for this!"

By the time I'd arrived at my dorm, he'd called three times but left only one message. He was crying, begging for forgiveness, promising that he'd never lay his hands on me again, pleading for my return.

"You took all your shit, ma. What's wrong with you? You're wiling! It's not that serious, *mamita*! We can work this out!"

He kept calling at least once an hour. With each message he

became increasingly irate. The last one was the worst.

You fucking sucia. You think you can get away from me?! This is the motherfucking infamous Fabian you dealin' with here, bitch! You'll never get away from me. I told you, you fucking cuero, you're mine forever, bitch! I will hunt you down like the fucking snake that you are! I will hunt you down and slice you to pieces! You hear me you fucking crazy bitch! Oh, you think you slick, right? Well, I'ma show you who's the slick one. I filmed you with your lesbian lover, máldita maricona! That's right. I fucking filmed you! I'ma show that shit to the whole fuckin' hood. Charge for tickets and shit. Make copies and sell that shit!"

Then he broke down and pleaded for my return.

"Ma, please don't leave me. Please! I need you! I'm bugging! I would neva hurt you baby! Neva!"

I then heard muffled sniffing and knew immediately that he was doing coke. "Never get high on your own supply," I sang shaking my head then the reality set in. "He filmed us! That son of a bitch filmed us! I can't believe his trifling ass!"

My phone rang indicating that I had a new message. I hesitated but listened to it in spite of myself.

¡Ay Dios! Where are you, mamita? I called your dorm and your

suitemate said you were taken away by ambulance. Where are you, ma? My God, I pray you're okay. The stupid bitch couldn't even tell me what hospital they took you to. I'm gonna go to St. Luke's since it's the closest one to Columbia. If you're there, wait for me. I'm on my way. Your papí is on his way. Wait for me ma, wait for me.

My entire body tensed fearfully. He's on his way?! I thought dumbstruck. I jumped out of the bed and immediately regretted my impulsiveness as piercing pain shot through my crotch, up my abdomen and down my legs. I almost keeled over but managed to keep steady by holding on to the bedrail for support. I carefully dressed myself. I opened the door, looked up and down the corridor and walked out as fast as I could, avoiding the waiting room area altogether. I didn't stop until I was in the safety of my dorm room, knowing that the guards would never permit anyone entrance unless they received verbal permission. I collapsed onto my bed, privates throbbing, heart beating hard against my breast, sweat causing my shirt to stick to my body. I'd eluded him ... at least for now.

8

I laid on the futon of my dorm room reminiscing about the last five years of my life. I remembered the day I hooked up with Fabian like it was yesterday.

I'd known Fabian for years. He hung out on the corner of the block where my Grandmother lived. I would walk by the group of guys and giggled at their comments on what a cute girl I was and a beautiful woman I was sure to become. But Fabian always took it further, following me, and telling me that he was going to marry me one day.

"You're gonna be mine. You don't know it or believe me now, *mami*, but you're gonna be my *princesa*. You'll see."

I was always flattered but also wary of this man. After all, he was eight years my senior. I was just a young girl of twelve, still learning to be an adolescent, but not even a teenager. How could he see so far into my future? How could he be so sure of himself? How did he know he could win me over?

Still, I found myself going to the corner store more often or out for walks to the park. I'd conjure up any excuse to pass by the corner so Fabian could stare at my pubescent body. The way he watched me made me feel special and wanted. I would put a little extra shake in my strut when I knew he was watching.

Fabian waited until I was seventeen to make his move. It was the summer before my senior year in boarding school and I was spending the last few weeks before the beginning of classes at my grandmother's house while my mom visited relatives in Puerto Rico. I befriended Lynette, a girl from the block, who shared my crush on Fabian. I came to find out that Fabian had a number of the girls in the hood crazy for him. We'd watch him drive by in his glossy black Mercedes Benz, vying for his attention but it was all too obvious that it was me he wanted. He'd only stop to flirt when I was standing on the block and when I wasn't, he'd stop to ask where I was and when I was coming back.

One stiflingly hot day, Lynette and I were on our way to the park when Fabian pulled up alongside us in his dope ride.

"I always knew you were going to be gorgeous but damn baby, you flyer than I ever imagined," he declared biting his lip seductively.

He stepped out of his car and approached us giggling girls.

"Who you talking to?" asked Lynette hopefully. "Me?" she asked enticingly pointing to her large bosom, "Or her?" She rolled her eyes and pointed at me apprehensively.

Fabian ignored Lynette and looked at me candidly. "When you gonna let me take you out, *mami*?"

While he spoke he put his finger through the belt loop of my fitted jean shorts. He looked at me up and down, licking his lips, undressing me with his gaze. I stepped back and looked at the ground shyly. My face flushed when he put his finger under my chin and pulled my face towards his. He kissed my forehead tenderly, slipped his number into the back pocket of my jeans, and copped a quick free feel of my tight bottom.

"Call me whenever, *mami*. Let me give you the world."

He backed up, opened the door to his car and stepped in smoothly, without taking his intent gaze off me. He blared Biggie & R. Kelly's *Fucking you Tonight,* blew me a kiss and sped off. Fabian knew what he was doing. He knew how to seduce a young, inexperienced girl who craved attention and love. I called him that very night.

I was supposed to be going to 42nd Street to watch a movie with Lynette or so I told my grandmother. Instead, Lynette and I took the A train to 181st and I called Fabian. He picked us up five minutes later. We dropped Lynette off at the theatre and I pleaded with her to cover for me. I provided specific instructions.

"If my grandmother calls, tell her I went to the bathroom or something and call Fabian right away." I punched Fabian's number into Lynette's cell. "Yo, look out for me, ma. My grandmother will have my ass if she finds out I lied to go out with this nigga."

"Don't worry, ma. You my girl. I got you," retorted Lynette but I sensed some resentment in her voice and could swear I saw her cut her eyes.

"I'll call you tomorrow with all the details," I assured, ignoring Lynette's spite.

"Oh, y'all gonna make a bitch take the train home? That's shady, yo," said Lynette with attitude while staring at Fabian slyly.

"You good, girl. You should be used to riding the train but here's some money so you can catch a movie, get something to eat and take a cab home." Fabian nonchalantly handed her a Benjamin. "Let me take your girl out and show her a good time. Get in the car, *mamita*," said Fabian, winking at me.

I gave Lynette a kiss goodbye and noticed that she didn't return the kiss. "Be happy for me please." I squeezed her arm, got in the car and drove off, leaving her sulking on 42nd and 8th Avenue.

Fabian took me to Tito Puente's seafood restaurant on City Island. There he insisted that I order the most expensive dish and slipped the waiter a fifty so he'd get us a bottle of Moet without carding me. I hadn't had a drink in my life and had never been treated to such a deliciously scrumptious, expensive meal. By the time we left, I was giddy from the alcohol and the endless praises Fabian whispered in my ear. He had me where he wanted – in the palm of his hand. Afterward, he took me to Fort Tryon Park where he sucked my juvenile breasts until they were raw. Despite the alcohol, I wouldn't let Fabian roam under my skirt.

"No, pa," I pleaded. "I'm a virgin, no. I'm not ready yet."

Fabian stopped and looked at me with a smirk, "Gives me something to look forward to." When he dropped me off a block away from my grandmother's house, he kissed me deeply. "I told you I would have you one day."

"You don't have me yet." I laughed nervously as I stepped out of the car. The truth was that he'd had my heart for years.

I skipped down the block on cloud nine. I couldn't believe I had an older man, a paid nigga chasing me. I chuckled nervously thinking about the way he kissed my lips and breasts. No one had ever made me feel so extraordinary, so sought after. I didn't remember the last time I'd been so elated. My face dropped when I saw my grandmother sitting on the stoop of the building.

"¿Y Lynnette, donde esta?" inquired my grandmother suspiciously.

"Oh ... um ..." I stuttered. "She stayed *hanguiando con unas amigas* but I told her my curfew was midnight."

"¡Mentirosa!" yelled my grandmother. *"¡Te fuistes a cueriar!"* She cursed me and dragged me inside by my hair, lecturing me in her thick Spanish accent. "Now ju can't go out for the rest of the *verano* and I'm gonna tell jour moder too! I'm gonna call her in the morning to tell her of your *perrerías*!"

I was horrified. I could deal with my grandmother labeling me a slut and smacking me up but the idea of being grounded for the remainder of the summer devastated me. I won't be able to see or spend time with Fabian!, I thought tearfully. And what happened to Lynette? I thought she had my back. I thought she was gonna cover for me. I cried into my pillow and didn't stop sniveling until I fell asleep.

The following day I awoke to find that my grandmother had left to work. I immediately picked up the phone and called Fabian. He answered groggily.

"Yo, who this calling me at this insane hour?"

I looked at the clock to see that it was already noon. "I'm sorry, pa. I'll call you later."

"No *mami*. I didn't know it was you, *preciosa*. Talk to me baby. I love to hear your voice."

I smiled briefly then started sobbing. I explained what happened when he dropped me off.

"It's alright, ma. Don't worry. They can't keep us apart. No one can. You call me whenever you want and we'll see each other some way, some how."

"But how? I can't even leave the house," I blubbered.

"We'll figure it out, ma. Don't worry and stop crying. I can't bear to hear you so sad. It breaks my heart, beautiful. As fine as you are though, you probably look devastating when you cry," Fabian said, making me giggle. "As for your friend, Lynette, she's a shady bitch. She hatin' 'cause she know you got my heart, ma. That's all. Don't sweat that bitch. Fuck her!"

"Nah, Fabe. Something must've happened. She's my best friend. She wouldn't do that to me," I responded defensively.

"She's trife, ma. Trust me. You'll see that I'm right. Just watch, you'll see."

When I hung up, I dialed Lynette's number but got her voicemail. I left her a message begging for her to call me back. Lynette called three hours later.

"Yo, my bad, ma. Your grandmother called and I was all high and silly, I didn't know what to say. I'm so sorry! What happened? Did you get busted?"

I explained what happened while Lynette listened anxiously. "Damn my bad yo!" apologized Lynette. "Yo, whateva I can do to help you out, let me know. And, don't worry, I'll keep an eye on Fabe for you and make sure he don't try to play my girl, aight. I'll call you later. Smooches!"

Naively, I didn't doubt Lynette's loyalty. I didn't understand why Fabian would say such mean things about her but I would find out shortly thereafter.

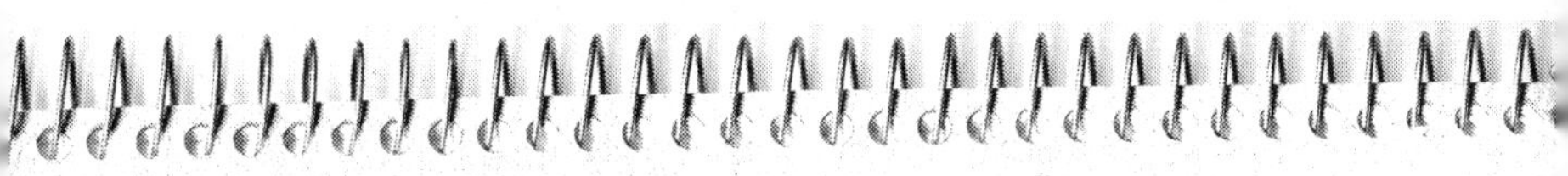

Fabian and I sneaked around for the remainder of the summer. He'd visit me when my grandmother was at work and we'd fool around until Fabian got blue balls. I held onto my virginity with an iron tight grip.

"I'm just not ready yet, pa," I'd explain when he'd try to go into my pants. He started calling me his number one cock-tease in jest but I knew that he was only half joking.

As promised, Lynette kept her eye on Fabian for me. She'd call me daily with updates. She even started hanging out with him "so I can keep a closer eye on him for you," she explained innocently. So whenever I heard murmurings that Lynette was messing with Fabian, I brushed it off and convinced myself that they cared for me too much to betray me.

During my last year at boarding school, Fabian periodically sent me money and care packages filled with expensive hair products, bath salts, and body lotions. In one package, he sent me a cell phone so I could call him whenever my heart desired. The rumors about Fabian and Lynette kept flying despite their assurances that they'd never hurt me in such a vile manner. I started calling Fabian round the clock to ease my worries.

On his first visit to Boston, before he was able to even put his luggage down in the hotel room, I confronted Fabian about my concerns. He flipped on me and manipulated me into feeling guilty for my "false" accusations.

"It's not like you're giving me any pussy so you couldn't blame me if I did fuck another bitch!" he yelled.

"So that's what this is about? I haven't put out so you have to go get it elsewhere, *desgraciado*!" I cried.

Fabian grabbed me by my waist and pulled me close to him, caressing me he said, "Baby, I told you I would wait as long you want me to. I am not playing you and I'd never play you but a nigga got needs, ma. I been holding out for you too, you know."

He cupped my face and kissed me intimately. He laid me on the bed and kissed my face and neck. Slowly, he removed my blouse and played with my nipples. I sighed with pleasure. The lower on the abdomen he kissed, the sharper my intakes of breath became and the more I tensed my body.

"Relax, *mami*, you tell me to stop if you want me to."

He started to kiss my crotch over my jeans, biting hard enough so I could feel him through the denim. I offered little resistance when he unzipped my fly and pulled off my pants. He put my clitoris in his mouth smoothly and allowed my facial expressions and body movements to guide him. When I tensed and parted my lips in ecstasy, he moved his tongue faster and harder. When he felt me cum, he took my entire cunt into his mouth and sucked, flicking his tongue in and out of my hole while I squealed in delight. When he came up for air, my *jugos* dripped from his chin. He cradled me in his arms.

"I told you I'd never hurt you baby. Neva, mamita. Neva," he repeated as he fingered me roughly. "Hold up." He slid off the bed and removed his pants and boxers.

I gasped at the sight of his erect penis. I'd never seen a dick so up close and personal and his looked immense to my inexperienced eyes. He laughed at the frightened expression on my face. "You act like you've neva seen a dick before, ma."

"I haven't. At least not in person. On cable but not face to face," I giggled. "And I've never had an orgasm either," I delighted as he slipped into bed next to her.

"You ready?" he asked as he rubbed my G-spot.

"As ready as I'll ever be," I sighed. I looked into his eyes and said what I'd been wanting to say for months. "I love you, Fabian."

"I love you too, *mamita*," he replied as he entered me with a single thrust. I yelped as he plunged into my tight pussy.

Fabian made it a point to come see me in Massachusetts as least once every two weeks. He also made certain my pussy was sore when he left. The rumors of Fabian and Lynette's affair subsided only for new gossip of his infidelities to arise. One day Lynette called me out of the blue. We hadn't spoken in a while so I was surprised to hear Lynette's voice on the line.

"Wow, girl, what's this miracle?" I inquired.

"Look, ma, I'm sorry I haven't called but I been busy. I just called to tell you that I think your man is playing you with some fifteen-year-old hoe from Post. I'm just tryin' to look out, aight."

"Oh, like you were tryin' to look out when you were up and down with my man?" I accused. "And now that he kicked you to the curb, you're lookin' out for me? That's absolutely hilarious!"

"What, bitch?!" Lynette yelled.

"No, you just didn't call me a bitch! You need to slow your role, Lynette, for real. See, that's why we ain't tight like we used to be. I just can't trust you."

"Can't trust me?" Lynette mocked. "But you trust your player man. You're the hilarious one, yo, not me. Now you go tell your man thanks for all the nuts, *pendeja*!" and she slammed the phone on my ear.

I was enraged. "No this bitch didn't just say that to me. She got the heart to admit to fuckin' my man ova the phone but when I confront her about it, she almost cried denyin' it?"

I called Lynette's phone repeatedly for over an hour but got no response. When I called Fabian's phone I didn't even wait for him to say 'Hello' before I went off on him.

"You nasty mothafucka! *¡Ásqueroso!* You fucked that bitch Lynette?!" I wailed. "How could you do that to me? After everything I've done for you. I gave you my virginity, you son of a bitch!"

"What?! You're wilin', ma! I didn't fuck that *cuero malo*! I told you that and I'm tired of you accusin' me. I don't have time for any of that shit, babe. Between maintainin' the spot and goin' to see you, I don't have time for anything! Calm down!" he tried to soothe me.

"That bitch called me and said she slept with you!" I hiccupped. "How could you, pa? Why? Why? Why?" I pleaded.

"Ma, I didn't. I swear, I didn't!" he vowed. "I would neva do that to you. Neva mamita, neva! I wanna marry you, babe. You my queen, I swear. Please stop cryin'!"

Lynette was only the first of a long line of females with whom Fabian played me. By accepting his betrayal and believing his crocodile tears, I'd set a precedent that I'd never be able to erase and would live to regret.

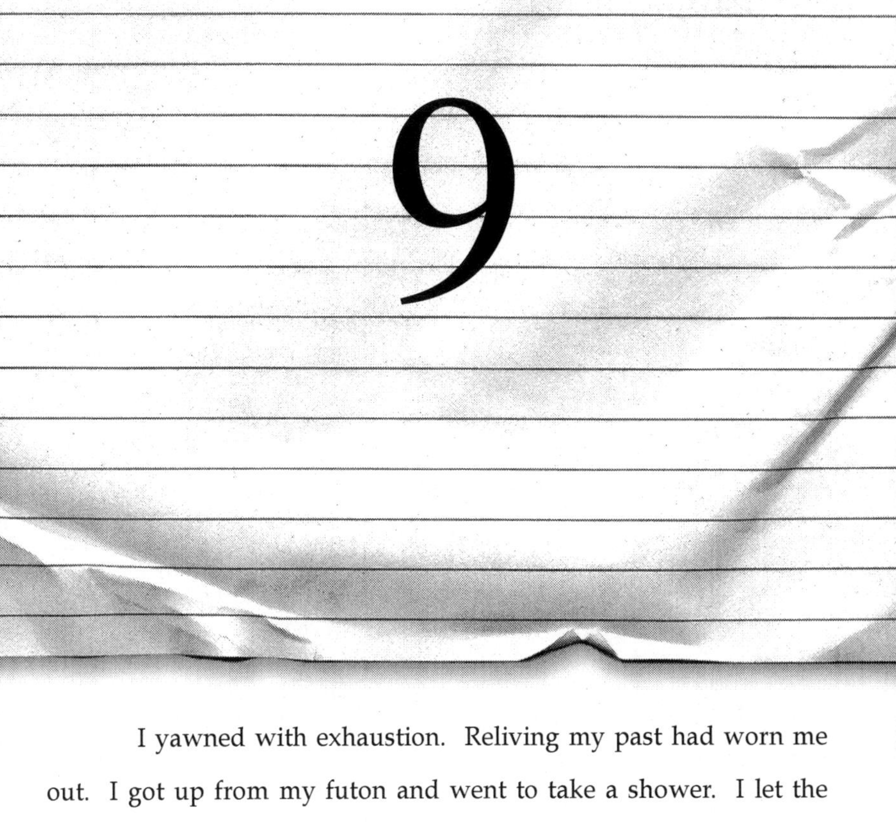

9

I yawned with exhaustion. Reliving my past had worn me out. I got up from my futon and went to take a shower. I let the hot water run over my face. When I lowered my head to wet my hair, I saw that I was still bleeding. Salty tears rolled into my mouth as I remembered the miscarriage I'd had two days earlier. I realized that I'd been able to avoid Fabian thus far but knew that my time was running out. I was going to have to face him eventually but still couldn't stand the sight of his face. I had a class in an hour and a half but couldn't fathom having to face reality just yet. I decided to skip it and take a long, hot bath. I ran the bath, threw in some bath salts and soaked my worries away. I tried to clear my mind but failed.

Thoughts of Fabian and my disillusionment wreaked havoc on my soul.

All my life I had dreamed of attending Harvard University. When I fell in love with Fabian that all changed. I didn't believe our relationship would survive the distance so I was overjoyed when I was accepted to Columbia University. Admittedly, I was nonetheless getting a topnotch education that would open doors for me in the future but I always wondered what life would have been like had I stayed in Cambridge and followed my lifelong aspiration. Instead, I had opted to follow my heart and here I was sulking in a tub, recovering from a miscarriage and the damage Fabian had inflicted on my body but my emotional scars ran far deeper than any of the superficial wounds.

I inhaled deeply hoping that the juniper aroma of the bath salts would serve to cleanse my spirit. My efforts were once again futile. Despite my attempts, my mind continued to wander back to the past.

I resentfully recalled the many times I had compromised myself and my beliefs for the sake of my love for an undeserving man. I couldn't count how many times he had played me, often right in front of my face. He'd even brought a girl to our home claiming she was an old friend. I befriended her, smoked Ls with her and talked to her, only to find out months later that she was actually one of his many lovers. Each and every time I discovered an infidelity, I vowed to leave him but each and every time, I took him back.

I became so insecure and distraught that I convinced myself

that if I shared in his passion for other women, it would be easier to deal with, that he wouldn't then have to go do it behind my back. So I proposed a threesome. Naturally he jumped at the invitation. I remembered clearly how revolted I felt the first time I saw him fuck another woman, so much so that in the middle it I had to run to the bathroom to vomit. I realized then and there that the way he fucked me was no different from the way he fucked all the other women he'd been with. For the longest time, I held on to the illusion that only I could spark such zeal and tenderness in him but that night, watching him kiss and caress that female, I saw that I had only been fooling myself.

The problem was that once I did it, I couldn't go back. Fabian demanded threesomes regularly. I was so *asfixiada*, so *entregada* that I obliged. I numbed myself with drugs and alcohol and did what he wanted, when he wanted. I sucked his dick while he ate an unfamiliar pussy. I performed felatio on a stranger while he fucked me from behind. Later, once the euphoria of the drugs had worn off, I would cry in the bathroom, running the shower so that he wouldn't hear my pitiful howls.

I often wondered how it was I was able to attend school fulltime and actually maintain an impressive GPA but, come what may, I did. Somehow I would zone out my pain and heartache and concentrate on the work at hand. I felt sometimes like school was my escape, the one place where I could free my soul of the manacles that was my obsession with Fabian. Despite how vulnerable and insecure

I felt, the one thing I depended on was my drive and dedication to my schooling and academic future. I always promised myself that I'd never let anything get in the way of my education. That was my one consolation – that I hadn't compromised my studies for anything or anyone.

I was only two months away from receiving my bachelor's degree. I vowed silently to myself that I would graduate on time, even if it killed me.

10

I jumped out of the bath. I had fifteen minutes to make it to my Writing Class. It didn't matter that the doctor in the ER had given me a note permitting me another day of respite. I had to go to class if I wanted to graduate on time. I ignored the stitch of pain in my front as I changed quickly into a Juicy sweat suit and ran out the door. As I sped to class, scanning the block for any signs of Fabian, I turned on my cell for the first time since being released from the hospital. My voicemail signal rang immediately, startling me so that I almost tripped. I put off hearing my messages knowing it was Fabian calling. I just wasn't ready to take that on. Instead, I called my best friend, James.

"What up, nena? I've been calling you. Why'd you have your phone off? Are you okay?" asked James nervously. James was all too aware of my abusive relationship. I didn't tell him everything but I shared enough for him to know that the partnership was unhealthy. Many times he'd lectured me about how I was selling myself short. He'd remind me of the bright future I had ahead of me and warned that Fabian was the only obstacle in my path. Simply put, I deserved better, there was no denying that.

"Yeah, I'm fine," I said almost inaudibly.

"Liar!" James knew me well enough to know when something was wrong. We'd met during our first year at CU and had become immediate friends. Of course Fabian disapproved of our friendship due to his irrational jealousy but I had maintained the closeness in spite of Fabian's condemnation. "Come through. Let's smoke an L and talk," James offered.

"I have to go to class. I'll call you when I get out," I replied with moistening eyes.

I was relieved to find that class had been cancelled. I was surprised because Professor Daines was known for holding class even if she was running a high fever and coughing up a lung. I immediately felt guilty when one of my classmates informed me that Professor Daines had sprained her ankle on her way to class.

"I hope she's okay," I mused worriedly.

Professor Daines was my favorite professor at Columbia. I'd taken a writing class with her every semester since my freshman year.

I loved the way she challenged me and demanded perfection and would call a student out if she saw that they were half-assing their work. I admired the way she brought out the best in her students. She wasn't just my professor, she was my mentor. She was the one that had put it into my head that I should consider a career in writing. Although I hadn't confessed to her that I was in a sadistic relationship, Professor Daines had picked up on it in my writing. "All fiction has a basis in reality," she often said. The professor didn't pry but always assured me that if I needed someone to talk to or anything at all, I could always feel comfortable coming to her.

As I walked out of Lewisohn Hall I became increasingly aggravated. This was the one time that I would have taken Professor Daines up on that offer. Now that I needed her, she had her own issues to deal with. Story of my life, I brooded miserably.

My warped relationship with Fabian had made me a guarded individual. I didn't feel comfortable talking to many people about my troubles so it felt odd to feel the need to talk to the professor. I knew, however, that I had no intention of talking to a stranger about it even if she was a licensed professional. That's why I hadn't opted to speak to the social worker at the hospital. If I were ever going to open up to anyone about my grief, it would have to be with someone with whom I had an established relationship.

I called James from outside his dorm, East Campus. "I'm coming up," I said.

"A'ight. Perfect timing. I'm rollin' an L."

I smiled as I waited for the elevator. I loved the shit out of James. I could always rely on him to make me laugh when I thought I couldn't. At times I felt he was too hard on me but sometimes that was what I needed without knowing it. When I sought a reality check, to be put in my place, I knew I could go to James. He never failed me and as I rode the elevator to the fourteenth floor, I realized that a dose of James was what I needed right then.

James's jaw dropped when he saw the bags under my eyes and my sallow complexion. "What the fuck happened?" he asked hugging me.

"Let's just smoke, please," I pleaded. "I'll tell you in a second. Let me just relax." I looked him dead in the eyes, hoping he would see the despair.

"No problem, ma."

He passed me the L and a lighter and I watched James as he prepared a Grey Goose with cranberry and squeezed a slice of lime into the drink. "It's a little early for a drink but it looks like you need one," he said laughing, making an effort to lift my spirits.

"Good lookin' out." I drank half the glass in one swallow.

"That bad, huh?"

I just sighed and lit the L. I took a deep drag and lay back as the grajo-smelling fumes filled my lungs. I immediately felt the marijuana-induced euphoria begin to take hold and took another puff before passing it.

I watched James as he smoked. He was a good-looking guy;

tall, lanky with thin lips, attentive eyes and a killer smile. If I'd met him in another lifetime, maybe, but I hadn't and I couldn't say I regretted that. He was my closest confidante, my boy and I couldn't fathom things being any different.

James choked on the malodorous ganja sending me into a fit of hysteria. The weed had calmed my nerves. I felt giddy and the most cheerful I'd felt in days. James chuckled in between coughs.

"So what's up, *nena*? Ready to talk?"

My mood became solemn. I took a deep breath and filled James in on the ghastly events of the past few days. I admitted that it wasn't the first time Fabian had laid his hands on me and told James of the many times Fabian had deceived and manipulated me. James let me speak without interruption, getting up only to pass me a handkerchief to clean my dripping eyes and nose, and to place himself next to me to console me as I vented.

When I was done talking, I felt like a huge weight had been removed from my shoulders. In a way, finally telling someone of what I had endured in the past five years freed me of the pain. I began the process of healing and redemption.

"So, what you gonna do?" asked James pointedly.

I looked at James in shock. For once, no 'I told you so's' or 'You shoulda known better's' came out of his mouth. James gazed at me with concern. I threw my arms around him and hugged him tightly.

"I need to leave him, James. For the sake of my emotional and physical health and my future, I need to walk away from him and not look back." I choked back the tears. "But I don't know where to start. I don't know how to leave."

"You leave by leaving, India, that's how," James said frankly. "You're stronger and smarter than you give yourself credit for. C'mon yo!" James stopped himself and shook his head. I sensed that he knew that this wasn't the time for hard-ass James. I needed him to be delicate. "What can I do to help, ma? Say the word."

I sat back and sipped my drink. I didn't know what to say. James took my glass and refilled my drink as if on cue.

"Thanks, pa." I stared at the glitter of the cubes in the cup. "You know, you're right. I'm stronger and smarter than I give myself credit for." I smirked as an idea dawned on me. "You ever notice how I've never worked in my entire college career?"

"Duh, your man or ex-man," he corrected with pride, "is a dealer. What the fuck you gonna work for?"

"True that. Well, I haven't spent all the money he's flossed on me either." I winked. James stared at me interested. "Yeah, I spent a lot of money in the past four years but I've also saved a lot of money too."

"How much is a lot?" James inquired with increased curiosity.

"Last time I checked about a month ago, I had $25Gs spread out over four accounts and I've deposited at least five to six more since then." I was feeling progressively more optimistic as I pondered the possibilities. "Plus you know Fabian knows nothing about financial management, right?"

"Typical uneducated drug dealer." James rolled his eyes and shook his head. "Pathetic."

"Well, when you in the streets, you make interesting connects. I have a connect at Bank of America that created several accounts for me. Under aliases, of course," I added to smooth James's arched eyebrows. "I made sure I have signatory rights on each and every account. He may be a dick and treated me like shit but I'm the only one he trusts with his money, James. Now I'm gonna use that to my advantage. There's well over 200Gs in those accounts. Maybe even three hundred. Plus I know the combination to his safe and where he keeps some of his money stashed."

As the alcohol and marijuana mingled in my blood and sharpened my high, the possibilities swirled in my head making me more optimistic and ready to take Fabian on. "That *hijo de puta* is gonna pay for what he's done to me. He's gonna regret the day he fucked with me. I'm gonna hit him where it'll hurt him the most - in his motherfuckin' pocket." I laughed heartily.

I picked up my cell phone. I was finally ready to face reality. I pushed the voicemail button and punched in my password.

11

Yo mamita, where the fuck are you? I went to the hospital and they wouldn't tell me shit. I call your suite and nobody fuckin' answers the phone. I call your cell and you have it turned off. I need to know if you're alive, ma. Oh God, please be alive!!!! Call me, please. I'll leave you alone if you want me to … just let me know you're okay.

For a brief moment, I actually felt bad for Fabian. It made me feel good that he was worried about me. I breathed deeply remembering how he'd treated me and every iota of remorse I'd felt left me quickly. I listened to his second message.

Yo, what the fuck?! You tryin' to run from me, bitch? Tryin' to hide? I hope you're fucking dead you dyke ho! If you're not, I'm gonna be the one to hammer the nails in your coffin, you fuckin' sucia! I always told you you'd never get away from me! I'm gonna hunt you down! I'll find you bitch! Don't worry! Enjoy it while you can 'cause when I get my hands on you, it's over for you son! YOU HEAR ME! OVER!

My heart battered my chest cavity. My hands shook as I grabbed a cigarette and lit it. James stared at me baffled. "Since when do you smoke cigarettes?"

I took a deep drag and almost choked. I passed James the phone without looking at him.

"Press 4 and listen."

James's eyes grew to the size of saucers as he listened open mouthed. He put the phone down slowly,

"I have a question. If he beat you before, how come I never saw you lumped up?"

"He's not exactly stupid, James. He'd always hit me below the neck where no one would see the bruises. And in the summertime, he made sure not to hit me on the legs so they wouldn't be marked up." I pulled up my T-shirt to expose the now greenish-blue bruises on my obliques and turned my body to show him the contusions on my back.

"Damn, yo. This nigga ain't playin'."

My mind went into high gear as I structured my plan. "I gotta do what I gotta do, James." I looked at him with fire in my eyes. "It's either him or me and it sure as hell ain't gonna be me."

"I don't know what you have planned ma but know this, I'm here for you. Whatever you need, I'm here. I can't let you go this alone. You my homegirl and I love you and couldn't bear to find out that something happened to you while I stood by idly."

I kissed James on the cheek and hugged him firmly.

"I know you got my back, babe. I gotta go. I'll call you."

James reached out to grab my arm. I recoiled defensively and almost swung on him.

"Whoa, whoa, it's me, India."

I gasped. "I'm sorry ... sorry ... I just..." I stood there looking at him shamefully. "This nigga's got my nerves on end. I didn't mean to..."

"I know, I know," James said holding me. "Just don't forget to call me. I'm gonna be breakin' my head wonderin' if you're okay."

"Got it. I'll call you soon. I love you, James." I stopped at the door to look back at him.

"I love you too, India. Be careful. Please take care of yourself."

12

I took deep, meditative breaths as I walked down 116th. I practiced my speech as I passed the Law School and approached Amsterdam Avenue. As I hailed a cab, I repeated my intended words over and over. I finally reached for my cell when I slid into the back seat.

"Tuckahoe and Cayuga Roads in Westchester County," I instructed the cab driver. "You can take the Deegan."

"That's gonna be about $50, ma'am," the driver interrupted rudely.

"I didn't ask you all of that!" I said throwing him a $50 bill. I rolled my eyes and dialed *67 before dialing Fabian's number.

"Hi baby."

"So you decided to call," Fabian said with an evil snicker.

"Look, pa, I needed some time away but ..." I stuttered.

"Where are you? And why the hell are you calling me from a blocked number?" Fabian asked quizzically.

"I lost my phone... Oh my God, you've probably been calling my cell. Damn babe, I'm sorry. I lost my phone when I left your house that day,"

"Damn, ma, I'm sorry too. Have you even checked your messages? I've been worried sick. Your suitemate told me you were taken to the hospital."

"Nah babe. I just got out of the hospital this morning. I haven't had a chance to check my messages. I was taken in because I fainted. Turns out I have a mad case of anemia. I gotta start taking care of myself." I lied, luring him into my web with my deception. I smirked silently feeling him fall for my game.

"I'll take care of you, ma. Where are you?"

"I'm on my way to the crib. I'll jump in a cab in a second. Will you meet me there?" I asked in the little girl tone of voice that made his knees weak.

"Of course, ma. I'll go get you a sopita and I'll be there in an hour, k? I love you, ma. I miss you like crazy."

"I love you too, pa. I'll see you soon." I hung up and smiled at the cab driver who was staring at me in the rear view with a disgusted look on his face. "I'm such a great fuckin' actress!"

13

I flashed the cab driver my middle finger as I walked into the building. If only this motherfucker knew what I've been through, he wouldn't be looking at me like I was a conniving bitch.

"Fuck him!" I said loudly. The doorman looked at me strangely. "Good afternoon, Mike."

"Good afternoon, Ms. Maldonado."

When I stepped into the apartment, I pulled my sweatshirt off quickly and began rummaging the place searching for Fabian's video camera and the bank books. I ignored the aches that throbbed through my torso as I looked through Fabian's drawers. I found the bank books in the secret compartment that he thought I didn't know about under the floorboards in the living room. I pocketed a wad of hundreds that was there as well, leaving just enough so that he wouldn't miss what I'd taken.

I stared at the five kilos of coke lying in the compartment and figured that adding the six I'd found in the cache in the foyer closet and the eight I'd counted in the safe, there was enough cocaine in the apartment to get him a lengthy prison sentence. That was good to know. I nodded my head, pleased with my findings. Plan B if necessary, but I hoped it wouldn't come to that.

I continued probing the apartment. I mulled over the keys I'd found. Fabian had always sworn to me that he didn't keep drugs in the apartment. "I'd never put you in danger like that," I recalled him promising. But there they were, keys upon keys of uncut cocaine. Thank God the apartment had never been raided. I would have been fucked, my future destroyed if the police had ever run up in there.

"This rat bastard is a sneaky motherfucker! We'll see who laughs last," I thought aloud.

I finally found the camera behind his sweaters on the top shelf of his walk-in closet. I sighed in relief when I saw that the tape of my tryst with Anais was still in the camera. "This motherfucker thinks he's smarter than me," I mused. "NOT!" I removed the tape, put it in my bag along with the bundle of Benjamins and hid the bag behind the couch. I quickly grabbed the bank books and scanned the pages I needed on the printer. I returned them to the stash and went to take a shower. While in the shower, I retraced my steps in my mind to make sure I had covered my moves. The only thing that would tip him off would be the missing tape of my rendezvous with Anais. I couldn't think of what to do though. I had to take the tape, there was simply no alternative.

I tensed as I heard Fabian walk into the apartment and shook my body trying to loosen up in preparation for the confrontation. "I'm in here, babe," I yelled. I turned my back to the shower door so the first thing he'd see was the contusions on my back. I hoped it would incite guilt. My plan worked.

I turned when I was sure he had seen the bruises and saw his eyes water as he entered the shower fully clothed. I pushed the feelings of remorse out of my mind, reminding myself yet again of what he had done and the plan I had in place.

Fabian kissed me softly then more passionately. He began to grope my body but I stopped him. "I have my period, pa," I cloaked the lie with a soft tone, "I don't feel too good. I feel weak babe, weak and tired."

"You look tired, ma." He brushed strands of hair out of my face, picked me up and carried me to the bed. "Rest ma, I'll bring you the *asopao de camarrones* I bought."

I lied back and suddenly felt very hungry. I hadn't eaten in well over 24 hours and hadn't even thought about it until that moment. I ate the soup slowly, savoring every drop.

"You need anything else?" Fabian asked guiltily.

"No, I just want you to lie next to me and hold me," I said

in my little girl voice and patted the bed. He smirked and conceded without hesitation.

I put my head on Fabian's chest and let the tears fall freely. Fabian heard me sniffle and pulled my face to his. "Why you cryin', mamita?"

"Nothing, babe, it's nothing."

But that was far from the truth. I was crying for so many reasons. I cried because despite what he'd done to me, I still loved this man. I'd sacrificed so much for him, endured so much. I cried because I knew that I had to walk away and although I was resolute in my decision, it still hurt me that things had to end in such an ugly manner. I cried because I never thought it would come to this, that I would have to be so devious, so conniving. I had to adopt his street mentality and it made me feel grimy but I knew that Fabian would never leave me alone. It was either him or me.

Fabian interrupted my thoughts. "Look, ma, I'm sorry for what happened the other day. I let my feelings get the best of me. I wiled out and I'm sorry. It's just that I love you so much." He buried his face in my hair and inhaled deeply. "I love everything about you. The way your hair smells, the little bump on your nose, your little waist." He traced my body parts. "Everything!" He looked deeply into my eyes and I did my best to hide my anguish. "You forgive me?"

At that moment, I was overcome by a powerful urge to punch him in the face, to pounce on him and pummel him the way he had done to me. The past five years flashed before my eyes. I jerked my face away in repugnance. Almost instantly, I calmed myself down and improvised.

"I'm sorry baby. I think I have an eyelash in my eye. Ay, it burns." I waved my hand frantically over my eye.

He pulled my face close to his and blew into my eye. It was tender gestures like this that made me fall in love with him all those years ago. It was his practiced manner of manipulation but I wasn't falling for it this time. I'd never fall for it ever again, I pledged.

"I forgive you, baby. Maybe we should go to couples counseling or something," I suggested.

"Whatever you want, *mami*. Anything for you, *princesa*, anything."

"You want something to drink?" I conspired. "A Jack and coke or a Long Island?"

"Why, you want something, babe?" He made a move to get up but I pulled him back onto the bed.

"No, pa, let me get it. I feel a little better now that I ate. I have to go to the bathroom anyway. What do you want?"

"A Jack and Coke, *mami*. *Gracias*."

I walked into the bathroom and shut the door behind me. "Why you shutting the door?" Fabian asked, irritation creeping into his voice.

"Here we go," I whispered. I raised my voice to reason with Fabian through the shut door. "Pa, I don't want you to see me changing my maxi pad. That's gross." I faked a giggle hoping he'd buy it.

"Aight, babe, do your thang."

I quietly opened the medicine cabinet and took out the sleeping pills. "How many should I give him? I don't want to kill him but I want him to be out for a while, a long while. I put four pills into the pocket of my Victoria Secret terry cloth robe and walked out of the bathroom. I blew him a kiss as I walked out to the bar. Inconspicuously, I put the pills in his drink and made sure they dissolved before giving it to him. He drank the glass in four large gulps.

"Damn, pa, were you thirsty?" I laughed thinking how easy he'd made that.

He laughed with me and pulled me close to him. I lay there until I heard him snoring then I got up and began preparing for phase two of my plan.

I stared at Fabian's sleeping form. He looked so peaceful. Looking at him, you wouldn't think he was a misogynist, so malicious and manipulative. I wondered if it was a consequence of his upbringing or was embedded in his genes. Knowing his mother, I knew it was a combination of both.

I hadn't spoken to Fabian's mother, Maria, in years but she was a hateful woman, very jealous with her son. She had the hysterically farfetched delusion that no one was good enough for Fabian and had always treated me like I was beneath her. I put up with it for Fabian's sake until I couldn't take it anymore.

One day, I came down with an awful case of gastroenteritis. I had to be hospitalized for a week and spent two additional weeks recuperating. Fabian asked his mother to look after me while he was out taking care of business (I later found out that he was actually fucking the next door neighbor the entire time and his mother knew about it and played along). Maria treated me like shit, complaining about anything and everything, even accusing me of feigning illness to get attention. I finally kicked her out when I overheard her confess to her friend that she had put a *brujería* on me and my sickness was a result of the hex. That night, after Fabian heard his crying mother's version of what happened, he punched me so hard in the stomach that I threw up blood and had to return to the hospital for another three days.

When I remembered that scene, I was again overcome by a strong impulse to bash his face with the heavy candleholder that sat conveniently on the night table not far from where he lay unconscious. I settled myself with a meditative breath. In part I blamed myself, after all, I did accept it and take him back into my life. I willed myself to think about all the hardships I'd endured, feeling that it would eliminate any lingering pangs of guilt I may have about what I was about to do.

14

I called James from the cab. "Phase One is complete." I laughed as I told him what I'd done.

"You crazy bitch!" James said flabbergasted. "Damn *nena,* that was fast. It's only four o'clock. You bounced from here only three hours ago. Yo, he rubbed off on you some, ma. You straight up gangsta! I wouldn't want to get on your bad side."

"I'll take that as a compliment." I was slightly offended. "I'm just doing what I have to do to survive."

"I know, I know." He sounded defensive.

"You still on my side?" I asked apologetically.

"No doubt. Just say the word."

"I'm gonna need to stay with you until school gets out, pa. There's no way I can stay at my dorm. I have to steer clear of that side of campus."

"Damn, that's gonna fuck up my game," James joked. "Say no more. You need help getting your shit together?"

"Nah, I think I got that covered. Thanks, James. I'll call you later."

As soon as I hung up, I dialed the number to my connect, Mario, at Bank of New York. I instructed him to transfer all the money from the accounts I'd set up into two new accounts with new aliases, social security numbers, the works.

"It's after banking hours," Mario interrupted. "This will have to wait until tomorrow."

"I don't have until tomorrow, Mario. You have to do this now. Take 10Gs for the inconvenience and your silence," I added generously. "I'll hit you off with more once I see that you've done everything I've told you and kept your mouth shut. I'll call you in three hours. Is that enough time?"

"I'll call you in two," Mario said quickly.

I hung up, looked out the window and prayed silently.

God, I know this is wrong but I have to do this to get this man out of my life. He has to feel what I've been feeling for the past five years. This is the only way. This is his weakness. Please let this work out for me. Por Dios, por favor!

15

I exited the cab in front of my dorm at 47 Claremont Avenue. I looked around warily, although I knew in the back of my mind that there was no way Fabian could have regained consciousness. The dose I gave him was guaranteed to have him out until at least the following morning. My nerves were getting the best of me. I fumbled with my keys and dropped them twice before finally getting the key in the door.

The guard looked at me strangely. "You okay, India?" he asked concerned.

"Yeah, just tired."

I rushed into my room and began to throw my best clothes into the Louis Vuitton luggage Fabian had bought me for our three year anniversary. Those were the good times, I thought nostalgically then corrected myself quickly, "What good times, girl? The honeymoon didn't even last that long." Once I fit everything I could, I scanned the room to make sure I'd gotten everything that I absolutely needed. "What doesn't fit and isn't necessary will have to stay, " I said with resignation.

I looked at the framed picture of me and Fabian during our trip to South Beach. I picked it up and stared at my fake smile. We'd taken the picture at Wet Willie's after spending the day at the beach where Fabian kept comparing girls to me, making it a point to tell me which chick had plumper tits, a tighter ass or firmer abs. I'd stared at Fabian in disbelief. He was sitting there with his beer belly sticking out shamelessly and had the audacity to tell me that there were flyer chicks than me. I chortled remembering the eight pack abs that walked by at that very moment. I couldn't help but stare as the guy's chiseled physique. Fabian noticed and turned beet red. I smirked at him without having to say anything further. He'd read it all over my face.

I tossed the picture onto the futon and frowned at myself. I'd actually considered taking the picture with me. "What the hell is wrong with you?" I scolded myself aloud. "Snap the fuck out of it!"

Before leaving I told my suitemate that she was welcome to anything I'd left behind.

"Where are you going?" she asked inquisitively.

I looked at the gullible *chinita* with sad eyes. "I just have to go, okay. Take what you want and take care," I said struggling with my luggage. I stopped in my tracks and looked back, "Oh and if anyone calls, you didn't see me leave and have no idea where I am."

I called James from outside my dorm. "Yo nigga, come down to help me with my bags. I'll be outside the Wien Gates in five minutes." I hailed a cab with my free hand.

"This is all your shit, yo?" asked James doubtfully when I arrived. "I know you, girl. You had to buy an extra closet to fit all your clothes. Where's the rest of it?"

"I grabbed only what I could carry, James," I answered as I unloaded the cab. "Whatever stayed, stayed. I got enough money now to re-up my wardrobe with the latest shit anyway so I am not stressin' it." I winked at James teasingly.

"True that, true that. So when you takin' me shopping?" James asked hopefully.

"Wanna go in a little while? I need a distraction and shopping is just the thing to do that."

"1-2-5?"

"Nah, too close and too exposed. Let's head downtown."

"Sounds good," James said grabbing the heavier bags.

Right then my phone rang. "Fuck!" I swore as I struggled with the luggage. My body still hurt from the brutal combination of the assault and the miscarriage and I hadn't really rested despite the doctor's orders so I was starting to feel it. I picked up just before the last ring. "Hello."

"The transaction is done," informed Mario proudly. "You got my silence but…," he hesitated uncomfortably. "India, this whole shit sounds suspect. I just want to make sure I'm not in danger or anything," Mario blurted quickly before he lost the nerve.

"Don't worry, Mario. Nobody knows you by name or face or anything. Your ass is covered. It's my ass I'm worried about. Keep quiet and you'll be rewarded nicely. I gotta go. I'll call you within the next 48 hours. If you don't hear from me, worry but worry about me, not about you. Like I said, you're good." I hung up and walked into the building simultaneously elated and relieved.

"Phase Three commences now," I said in a robot-like voice making James look at me strangely and laugh.

"It's mad late." I was surprised as I looked at the clock marked 6:30pm.

"Too late to go shopping?" James asked with eyebrows arched.

"I see what's on your mind." I giggled. "This is New York, nigga, of course not. We can hit up 8th Street in the Village. Hurry up though. They're open late but not 24 hours."

James got ready in record time and we sped out the door. I relished in going from store to store, buying bags and bags of shoes, tops, jeans, dresses and whatever caught my fancy. I spent money on James without hesitation. He enjoyed it but stopped me when I readied to buy him a $500 pair of Gucci shoes.

"Nena, you don't have to do that. I'm already feeling guilty that you bought me all this." He gestured to the packed bags he was already holding.

I looked at him in the eye. "Listen, you my boy and I want to do this for you. I don't know what I'd do without you right now. It's the least I can do."

"I'd do it even if you were dead broke and homeless," James remarked honestly.

"I know." I gave him a peck on the cheek and took out my debit card. "Ch-ching!" We shopped until our feet throbbed and all the gates were drawn on the boutiques.

"I'm famished," I said. "You?"

"I could definitely go for some grub." James rubbed his flat belly. "Chinese?"

"No doubt. Chinatown is right there. Let's go."

I plopped into the seat at the restaurant. I'd wanted to go to the Seafood Palace where Fabian used to take me but thought twice about it. The food was off the hook but not worth my neck.

"So ..." James said looking at me over the top of the menu. "Have you thought about the consequences of your actions, India? Ain't no nigga gonna have the bulk of his money taken without reacting."

"I know, I know." The truth was I hadn't really thought it through. All I had focused on was revenge. I wanted that nigga to feel the anguish I'd felt and the best way to do that was to hit him in the pocket.

"Trust me, I didn't take even half of his money. He has a lot of it stashed in different apartments and spots."

"You still took a lot of his dough."

"I know. I just thought I'd hide out for a while and ..." My voice trailed off as I realized the enormity of my actions. It hit me like a ton of bricks. My hands began to sweat profusely and my heart flogged my breast. "Oh my God!" I brought my shaking hands to my face.

James grabbed my hands and cradled them. "We're gonna figure it out together, *nena*. Chill, I'm here. I got you. We'll put our heads together and figure it out."

I became nauseous when I smelled the heaping plates of Lo Mein, garlic shrimp and rice the waiter placed in front of me. I'd completely lost my appetite.

16

"Does he know your schedule of classes?" asked James softly. I had my head on his shoulder and was staring at the bag of food on my lap. I hadn't eaten anything. I turned to look out the window as the cab sped uptown. The high of shopping and lacing myself had long left me. I was just staring into space wondering how Fabian was going to react, what he was going to do. I shuddered at the thought of what he was capable of.

"India, think!" James raised his voice to get my attention. The cab driver glanced at us apprehensively through the rear view. James's glare made him look away quickly. "I know this is scary but what's done is done. Now you have to take action to protect yourself.

Does he know your schedule of classes?" I could see in his eyes that James's logical mind was churning, going through scenarios and possibilities.

"Nah, he never cared enough about my education to know things like that," I replied truthfully.

"Aight good. Does he know where I live?" There was a tinge of fear in his voice.

"Nah, he doesn't know that either."

James sighed uneasily. "You have to lay low, India. You go to class and come straight back to the crib. No hanging out, no more shopping, nothing. If you need anything from outside, I'll get it for you. Sorry *nena* but you gotta play hermit for now."

"I know, James. Thanks." Before realizing what I was doing, I kissed James on the lips then pulled back quickly, gasping at my loss of composure. "Yo, my bad. I just ..."

"Don't apologize. I understand. You're scared." James smiled. "I've been wanting to do that for four years," he added almost inaudibly.

I stared at James. My one consolation right now was that I had him to lean on. I knew he wouldn't abandon me and didn't worry that he'd take advantage of my vulnerability. We held one another silently for the remainder of the ride.

17

The glare of the sun shining on my face woke me before 8am. I wiped the sweat off my forehead and glanced around the room. James was standing at the foot of the bed, bare-chested in boxers drying off his back. "You're looking buff these days," I said surprised by James's cuts.

He laughed. "I just got back from the gym 20 minutes ago.

"Damn, why didn't you wake me up?" I threw him a pillow playfully.

"You were finally sound asleep. You tossed and turned all night. Bad dreams?"

He walked over and sat on the bed next to me. I sat up on

the bed and stared at him. I knew James was cute but I hadn't seen him topless since we'd gone to South Beach for spring break the year before. I squeezed his pec.

"Let me find out. I didn't know you had all of this." I traced his newly chiseled bicep and gave him a peck on the cheek. "Somebody's been hitting the iron. Seriously though, I would have loved to work out. I need the adrenaline but you're right, I did have nightmares." I remembered the dream I had with Fabian. He'd found me.

"Breakfast?" James asked as if he knew I needed to be distracted from my thoughts.

"Mmmm, sounds good. Menus?"

"Nah, how about I make you breakfast? How's egg whites with bacon, toast, OJ and coffee?" James offered.

"Let me find out. I would have moved in sooner if I knew I'd be getting this kind of treatment," I teased as we walked to the kitchen. We talked while James cooked.

"So, has he called yet?" James lightly buttered the pan for the eggs and stared at me with arched eyebrows.

"I turned off my phone last night and haven't checked my messages but if he finally woke up, I know there's a hostile message patiently waiting for me." I tried to shroud my fears with jest. "I'll check after breakfast. I don't want to spoil the mood." I punched James on the arm playfully.

After eating, James rolled an L for dessert. We smoked silently for a while.

"So, have you thought about what you're going to do?"

"I'll think about it after we smoke," I responded a little annoyed.

"Look, I'm sorry, ma, but you have to think about it now. It's not going to miraculously go away." James paused and collected himself when he saw my eyes moisten. "Yo, I don't mean to lecture you but I'm worried about you. Let's see where we're at? If he called, we can proceed from there, aight, *nena*?"

"We?"

"Yes, we. I told you you're not in this alone. This is our problem, not just yours."

For the second time in two days, I wanted to kiss James but I didn't. I'm buggin, I thought. I picked up the phone and dialed my password.

What the fuck did you put in my drink, bitch? You scheming? Bring it!

The composed tone of Fabian's voice worried me. I knew this was the calm before the storm. I stared at James blankly as I passed him the phone.

"So he's onto you," James said in between totes to the roach he held with tweezers. "That's no surprise. What now though?"

"I don't know but I can't stay hiding here forever," I said desperately as I paced the room.

"And where are you going, India?" James asked seriously.

He stood in front of me. "You gonna go face him? And tell him what? I took your money nigga?!" His breath deepened. "India, you're strong and all but don't be stupid. He'll kill you on the spot."

"But I have to do something!" I had barely finished my thought before James was in my face pleading.

"Do what, India? You're gonna get yourself killed! Think about it."

I backed up when I saw the redness of his eyes. "You're right. I just don't know what to do, James." I teared.

"I know *nena*, I know." James reached out, took me into his arms and rocked me. "For now, you can only go to class. As soon as you get out, it's back to the crib. We don't know if he knows about the money yet. He'll probably let you know when he does with one of his friendly messages," James joked trying to soften the mood. He looked me in the eyes. "Ok?"

"I guess I have no choice. I just have to wait it out."

"When's your next class?"

"Noon to two."

"Okay, I'll walk you, go to my class, and then pick you up. We can get take-out and come home." He hugged me and kissed the top of my head.

"So you're my bodyguard now?" I teased. "How about I make us dinner? Baked chicken with baked sweet plantains and yellow rice with corn. A green leaf and spinach salad lightly sprinkled with olive oil and balsamic vinegar with a dash of salt." I boasted my cooking skills.

"Damn, if I knew I was going to get this treatment, I would have had you move in earlier," James kidded. We looked at one another for a moment. I finally broke the awkward silence.

"I need the distraction and want to flex my culinary talents. So is it a date?" I flirted half playfully.

"Is it?"

"Let me go to the gym for a while. My legs could use some squats and lunges." I saw where the conversation was going and had to nip it in the bud before it went there.

"Gym? Girl, you just had a miscarriage and were beaten up by your ex. You go to the gym and you're going to pass the fuck out on the treadmill." James massaged my shoulders while he held me in front of him. "Ma, I know you have crazy nervous energy right now but you have to relax. We have almost two hours before class, how about another L?"

"Sounds good to me but I still could use a workout."

James patted me on the butt as we walked to the room. He smirked devilishly when I swatted him on the back of the head. "Men!"

18

I became increasingly restless as the unseasonably warm weather held and I remained cooped up in James's suite. The farthest I went was to class and the library then back I ran to the dorm, looking over my shoulder constantly. Two weeks lapsed and I hadn't heard from Fabian except for that frighteningly relaxed message. Perhaps I should have been relieved but I was far from reassured by his silence. Fabian was calculating in his malice. I knew firsthand how patient he was when he prepared to dole out his vengeance.

I recalled three years before when a childhood friend of Fabian's foolishly thought he could trick him into believing he'd been stuck up for a large shipment of kilos of cocaine Fabian had given him on consignment. Carlos's story was that he'd been accosted when he'd gone to make a sale. Fabian had made his boy think he believed him. Meanwhile, Fabian did some investigating of his own. He found that Carlos had actually sold the keys to some dealers in Washington Heights. The dealers were familiar with Fabian and his work. They knew without a doubt that it was Fabian's work because no one in the hood could get such pure, uncut coke but him. Fabian let Carlos sleep. One night, months after the alleged theft, they went out on the town. They hit up several clubs, popped mad bottles of Cristal and Moet then went to soak up the alcohol with plates of paella and lobster at Jimmy's Bronx Café. There, they were involved in a shootout where Carlos was left a paraplegic and Fabian came out miraculously unscathed.

Fabian swore up and down to me that he had not schemed the whole thing. "I was with that nigga the entire night. How could I have been involved?" But I knew Fabian better than that. I felt it in my heart. My gut instinct told me that the shooting was Fabian's doing. When we discussed it, I saw the disappointment in his eyes, in the frown lines on his forehead and around his mouth; he'd wanted Carlos dead.

I put down the book I'd been reading and walked to the window overlooking Morningside Drive. That was my usual spot now. If I wasn't in front of the TV, lying on the sofa reading, or on the computer typing a paper, I was sitting by the window staring longingly out at the street.

My heart suddenly skipped a beat. "Hasn't that car been sitting in the same spot for several days now?" I mulled, staring at the closing sunroof of the black Land Rover, its windows tinted the ebony color of the car. "That car does look familiar," I thought aloud as I puffed on the cigarette. My nerves had got me smoking, a habit I'd never imagined I'd pick up. I looked down at my quivering hand and shook my head. "You need to fuckin' relax, India! You're buggin' the fuck out. You don't know that car and it has not been there for days!"

"Talking to yourself now," James laughed as he closed the front door behind him. I jumped, turned ghostly white, and dropped the ashtray in the process. "Damn *nena,* you're mad jumpy. It's me, James. Remember me. I brought you some food and a fresh bag of herbals." He proudly pulled out a Ziploc sandwich bag packed with green and purple buds.

"You love me." I walked to him and planted a firm kiss on his cheek.

"So what'd you see outside that got you screamin' on yourself?"

I stared at the curl of smoke rising from of James' mouth. He's got nice lips, I thought to myself. "Oh, it was nothing, I'm just wilin." I took the L and inhaled deeply, taking too much smoke into my lungs. I struggled not to choke but lost the battle. I coughed harshly.

"There no such thing as nothing right now. If something makes you suspicious, it's your instincts telling you something.

What's up?"

I told him about the Land Rover and we walked over to the window together to look. "It was parked right there," I said pointing at the now empty spot. "I thought I'd seen it there for a couple of days but ... I told you I'm just jittery right now."

"Aight *nena*. I'm just checking." James looked at me tenderly. "How 'bout we hit the gym?" He pinched my waist playfully. "I see you gettin' a little soft."

I punched him on the arm, "Fuck you nigga! But the gym sounds great. I need a break from the monotony that's been my existence for the past two weeks!"

I went into the room and changed into one of my new Juicy couture sweat suits and a pair of Nike Shox sneakers. "Let's bounce!" I announced energetically. "I love workin' out when I'm high. I get into the zone!"

We walked over the bridge spanning Amsterdam Avenue. I looked down at the traffic while we walked. As I turned away, I could swear I'd seen the same black Land Rover out of the corner of my eye but it was gone when I looked again. I'm truly losing my mind, I thought, trying to slow my quickening pulse.

"I need this work out, J. It'll do wonders to calm me down."

"Yeah, you've been mad tense but that's understandable."

I hit the squats hard and did more lunges than I probably should have. I felt a cramp in my abdomen while doing my last set of leg lifts and decided to call it quits on my leg workout. I put on my I-Pod, jumped on the treadmill, and ran to the hard bass of my designated workout music, letting the adrenaline take me soaring.

19

I got out of the shower and stretched my arms. I looked at my naked curves in the mirror and smiled. "Not bad, Ms. Thing." Winking at my reflection, I wrapped my robe around my body and a towel around my wet hair before walking into the kitchen.

"Damn, it's about time girl! You were in there for an hour." James passed me a protein shake. "Having fun with my showerhead?"

"Shut up!" I gulped the drink. "Mmmm, strawberry-banana. Tasty!" I noticed James watching me as I took the towel out of my hair and let it cascade over my shoulders. I grinned as James's eyes roamed my firm legs.

"You could use a pedicure," James pointed at the chipped polish on my toes.

"Shut up! Like I've had a chance to go get myself primped." I walked over to the couch, sat down and turned on the TV. I flicked the channels absentmindedly.

"I gotta stretch. That work out got me crazy tight," I stretched my arms in front of me.

"I got you, ma. Let me flex my masseuse skills." James walked over and placed himself behind me.

"Mmmmm." I moaned as James went to work. His mother had attended the Swedish Institute for Massage Therapy and had practiced what she'd learned on James. He'd picked up on it easily and had used his expertise to seduce many a female.

I tensed when I felt James's heavy breathing in my ear. He pushed my hair to the side and began to kiss the back of my neck while his hands kneaded softly. He pulled my robe down to expose my bare shoulders. I quickly put my hand to my chest, holding the front of the robe so as not to reveal my breasts. James pulled his mouth away from my neck as if sensing my hesitation. He continued to rub, making his way down my back. I jumped when I felt his tongue run up my spine and bit my bottom lip as James nibbled on the nape of my neck. He grasped my shoulder tenderly, turned me around and peered into my eyes.

"We can't ..." I began but before I could finish, he took my mouth into his, gently at first, then more forcefully as he felt me acquiesce. We stared at one another as he opened my robe to reveal my ample bust.

He kneeled in front of me and took my breasts into his mouth. I cupped James's face and ran my hands over his head. I traced the back of his ears as I watched him, each lick and nibble purposely gradual and subtle. James brought his face to mine and lined my cheekbone and forehead with kisses. He teased my mouth with his and laid me down as our tongues tussled heatedly. He began to grind against me, pulling my legs up around his waist.

I quivered with pleasure as James lined my ribs and abs with open mouth kisses. I stared at the ceiling in disbelief and excitement. I can't believe this is happening, I contemplated silently. But he definitely knew what he was doing. I gasped when I felt him suckle my clitoris. I hadn't even felt him push my robe aside.

I pushed myself up with a forceful jolt, catching James's arm before he fell off the couch. My eyes beseeched him. "I'm sorry, pa. I just can't. We can't..."

"It's alright." James put his hand over his crotch trying to hide his hard-on. "I'm sorry ... I shouldn't have ..."

"It wasn't just you. It's not like I put up a violent struggle. I just... I would never want anything to get in the way of our friendship, James. If we went there and it didn't work out and I lost you, I don't know what I'd do. Please understand."

"I do. I know ... My bad," he said dejected.

"I have to get ready for class." I stood up and tied my robe tightly. "Another month and a half and we'll be walking across that stage."

"I'll walk you to class." He got up and stood in front of me. "I'm really sorry. I'm not tryin' to take advantage of you, India. I know you're vulnerable and all… I just… I couldn't help myself."

"It's all good. You're a great kisser." I poked him in the ribs. "Now I see how you got all these CU chicks crazy." I walked towards the bedroom.

"I love you," James said almost inaudibly. It wasn't the friendship 'I love you's' we'd always give one another. This was a heartfelt I'm in love with you "I love you."

I whipped around. "What'd you say?"

"Nothin'. I mean, I said I love you." He changed his tone.

"Oh, I love you too, pa." I walked over and hugged him tight.

As I was changing my clothes, I wondered if I had heard what I thought I'd heard. "Nah, there's no way … Great, another sign that I'm going insane!"

When James dropped me off in front of Hamilton Hall, I stared at him as he walked away. When he glanced back, I saw this gloomy, rejected look that I'd only seen on James's face once before – when his girlfriend of four years had suddenly broken it off.

20

The next two weeks crawled by at snail's pace. I went to class and walked back home as I had for the past month. I hit the gym religiously, trying to keep my mind occupied and off of Fabian's continued silence.

One day after working out, James and I walked back home quietly. We had thus far deliberately avoided the topic of our encounter. I noticed a change in the way he treated me. He still walked me to and from class and joined me at the gym but he had clearly distanced himself. He barely spoke to me except to periodically ask if I'd heard from Fabian or if I'd noticed anything irregular.

As we walked by the law school, I noticed a black Land Rover parked in front of the Wien Gates. I could just make out a figure through the darkly tinted windows. Wide, stocky shoulders made the driver appear to be a male but I couldn't be sure. As we got closer, the car screeched off, made a U-turn and stopped at the red light on Morningside Drive. I bolted down the block after the car. My instincts told me there was something ominous about the way the car tried to evade me, but the light turned green before I reached the corner and the car turned north and shot up the block before I could even read its license plate.

I turned around frustrated and saw James panting as he approached. "What the fuck was that about? You ran down the block doin' 60! What happened?" He looked flustered and out of breath.

"You need to hit the treadmill, pa. You're slow and your lungs need the cardio," I mocked.

"You're right." We stared at one another, both obviously happy that the tension had been eased for the moment. "So, what happened? What caused you to fly off like that?"

"You didn't see the Land Rover? You didn't see the way it sped off when we approached? It just seemed suspect. You told me to follow my instincts so I did."

"So, did you see the driver or catch the license plate?"

"Nah," I replied aggravated. "I didn't see shit! The tints are too dark and the car turned before I was close enough to read the license plate."

"You sure it's not your nerves getting to you, ma?" James

asked.

"Something tells me this is more than a case of jumpiness, pa."

"Aight, let's keep our eyes peeled. In the meantime, let's go smoke an L and get some dinner. I'm starving and this monkey on my back is beating the shit out of me." We laughed and walked arm in arm back to the dorm.

21

I stared longingly out the window as we smoked. The buzzing doorbell snapped me out of my thoughts. The smell of curry filled the room as James paid the delivery guy and walked over to me with the bag of Indian food.

"I wish we could go eat this on the South Lawn," I said depressed. "It's gorgeous outside."

James stared at me then suddenly his face lit up. "How's this? Go to the room and wait there for fifteen minutes, then take the elevator up to the last floor and wait for me outside the entrance to the stairs."

"What are you planning in that sick head of yours?" I asked

curiously.

"You'll see." He led me to the bedroom. "Fifteen minutes. No more, no less."

I paced the room wondering what James was planning. I couldn't figure it out so I sat on the bed and stared impatiently at the clock until fifteen minutes had passed. When I walked out of the room, I searched the apartment for clues but found none. I noticed that the food was gone and my stomach grumbled in consternation.

I took the elevator to the 20th floor and saw James waiting for me by the stairwell. "Ready?" he asked as I approached.

I wrinkled my nose and smirked. "This better be good."

James led me to the roof of the dorm. My mouth fell when I saw his surprise. He'd laid out a green blanket and prepared a picnic for us. He'd even lit candles but "the damn breeze keeps turning them off," he said discouraged.

We sat under the warm evening sun and ate. When we were done, I rolled an L.

"I have a question. How did you get the roof doors to open without setting off the alarm?"

"Ma, I'm an engineer," James flaunted. "It wasn't even that difficult. Just cutting some wires and shit. No biggie."

"Oh, so I see you've done this before. So how many of these CU chicks have you brought up here? I've heard rumors about you and your fan club," I teased.

"Actually, you're the first girl I've brought up here. I've come up here several times with the guys to smoke and drink but never with a female." I looked at him doubtfully. "Nah, I'm serious. Why would I lie?"

James had one last surprise. He reached into the picnic basket and brought out a bottle of Moet champagne and a basket of strawberries. "Can't have a picnic without the bubbly."

I looked at him shocked. "All this for me, pa? I don't deserve you."

"You deserve the world, India." He looked at me when he said this to ensure that I saw he was dead serious.

We sipped and smoked for a while in silence, soaking in the sun's rays. I tried not to feel attracted to James. I'd been fighting these feelings for weeks but it was undeniable; there was something there. I leaned over and put a strawberry to his mouth. Our eyes locked as James took a bite and I brought my glass to his lips. "Mmmm," he purred licking his lips. "You put me on to this."

I saw him hesitate and wondered what was going through his mind and why he pulled away.

"Put you onto what?"

"That bourgeois shit of champagne with strawberries. That's your shit. You the classy chick, not me." We laughed heartily.

I realized that he just wasn't going to open that door to me again. I exhaled deeply and lied back on the blanket. Feeling hot, I took off my fitted t-shirt and laughed at James's ogling.

"It's just a bra, James. No different from a bikini top."

"Sexy bikini top," James laughed. "Hmmm, let me see. That's from Victoria's angel collection, right? The embroidered bandeau style."

I burst out laughing. "You are hilarious! Somebody's a Victoria Secret connoisseur!"

We drank and smoked while we watched the sun set. When the stars began to dot the sky, James showed me the constellations and planets. "Unfortunately, we're in the city so the pollution makes it impossible to see all the stars. Upstate, in the campo, you can see millions of them. Makes you realize how small you are in the grand scheme of things." James stared up dreamily.

I watched James while he looked towards the heavens. I felt so tempted to kiss him, it was killing me but I'd lost my chance. *¡Sángana!* I scolded myself silently. I got up, walked to the ledge and looked down. I felt James come up behind me. He pulled me close, put his nose to my curly hair and inhaled. I wrapped my hands around his and we rocked slowly looking at the lights of east Harlem.

"I've wanted you since the first day I saw you four years ago," James whispered suddenly in my ear. I let him speak feeling that he was confessing something that he'd held in for far too long. "It was freshman orientation. You were standing in front of Butler library on line waiting to get your orientation package. You were wearing a white flowered summer dress and your hair was straight. You mesmerized me by the way you brushed it out of your face with a slight movement of your neck. You were still untainted, still innocent and naïve. That punk hadn't broken your spirit yet. I almost tripped over myself when I saw you moving into the same floor as me in John Jay Hall. I swore it was meant to be until I saw that dick comin' to your room every night. That's why we didn't meet until later. I was too glum to introduce myself."

I turned around to look at him, "I didn't know ..."

"Shhhh," he said putting his finger to my lips. "You know, you're the reason Lorena left me. She could sense the way I felt about you, she would watch me watch you. She couldn't take it and demanded that I end our friendship. When I refused, she left me."

I was taken aback by the admission. I'd never had any idea but then again, the fact was that I'd never left myself open to the idea. I'd always been so wrapped up in Fabian that I hadn't bothered to see what was right in front of me.

"You know I didn't know," I said shaking my head. "I had no idea ... I ..."

I didn't bother to finish my thought. I captured the moment without hesitation, cupped his face with my hands and kissed him. We stayed at the ledge making out for what seemed like an eternity, our tongues wandering each other's mouths as if searching for a lost pearl.

I led him to the blanket, gazing longingly at him while I did so. I took off his shirt before I laid him down and straddled him. Reaching back with one hand I unsnapped and removed my bra, then leaned forward so he could take my breasts into his mouth. I grinded him, feeling him quickly grow rigid as a roll of quarters, surprised by his size and width. Moaning, I reached down and played with myself while he suckled me. Then suddenly, he flipped me over and got on top of me. I resisted, "No…"

Again he hushed me. "I've been waiting for this for so long. Let me do it my way."

He kissed my brow and ran his fingertips lightly down my abdomen, sending shivers up my spine. He unzipped my pants with his teeth, staring at me the whole time. When he took my pants off, he sucked my bikini line teasingly. He started off slow, licking my vagina inch by inch. He looked at me before he took my clit into his mouth, "You ready?" he teased.

I saw stars as James went to work. He alternately flicked his tongue on my clitoris at lightning speed then massaged it from top to bottom, always hitting the spot at the right moment. When he felt my body tensing ready to orgasm, he put his finger into me and put pressure on my G-spot, sending ripples throughout my body. I threw my head back and screamed his name. My back arched and body wriggled. I tried to pull away, the intensity too much for me, but he wrapped his arms around my legs and held on, devouring me, making me have multiple orgasms.

"Oh my God," I shrieked.

When James finally stopped, I was dripping with sweat. We kissed longingly, then I flipped him over suddenly.

"My turn!" I arched my eyebrows mischievously.

I took his pants off and had to catch my breath when I saw his large member. "I'm impressed," I winked, making him laugh proudly, then I straddled him. I grabbed his cock and asked, "You ready?," as I tantalized him.

I rubbed his dick on my pussy making him moan desperately. When I took him into me, we both gasped with delight. I reached down and stimulated my clitoris while I rode him, first slowly then rigorously, enjoying the contorted expression on his face. He grabbed my ass and guided me up and down on his dick. I threw my head back in ecstasy. When I came, he pushed inside me so I could feel all of him. As my spasms slowed, I slid off him exhausted.

"Oh, this ain't over yet, *nenita.*"

I yelped playfully as he picked me up in the air and fucked me standing up. I held on to his neck and kissed him while he pumped me. He carried me to the ledge, turned me around and pounded me doggy style. He reached over and gyrated my clitoris while he drew into me. I moaned loudly, "I'm cumin' again baby, again ... Right there, right there!" My yelps made him pulse my clit faster and fuck me harder. I saw stars and collapsed onto the ledge in orgasmic shivers.

I turned around and took him into my mouth. He fisted my hair as I stroked the head of his penis with my tongue, licking it from top to bottom first then taking him entirely into my mouth. I sucked down the shaft and back up slowly initially then quickened when I felt his veins throbbing. Tightening my lips around his dick, I began to jerk him with one hand and played with his ball with the other. I could hear him gasping, moaning "Yes, yes" while I fondled him. When he came, I took him entirely into my mouth then pulled out so he could squirt all over my chest while I masturbated him. I watched him with his mouth open and eyes closed as he came all over me. He collapsed onto his knees in front of me and gazed into my eyes.

"I love you, India. I've loved you for so long…"

I hesitated, eyes filling with tears. Before I could utter a word, he kissed me intensely. "You don't have to say anything. Just know that I'm in love with you." He led me back to the blanket where he cleaned me off and cradled me. We lay there naked, holding one another until a cloud covered the moon and it started to drizzle. "Wanna go downstairs now?" he asked in a low tone.

"Not yet." I grabbed his hand and walked him to the exit. "Round two," I murmured. I licked his neck and kissed him as the rain began to fall.

He sat down, leaned against the door and I climbed onto him. I pushed him slowly into me and rode him in circles while he caressed my breasts. James licked the rain off me as it began to fall in cascades. We devoured one another, pulsating to the rhythm of the falling water. He pushed deeper into me begging, "Let me come inside you." He groaned loudly as I wriggled my hips, trying to take him even deeper. I felt his dick pulsate as he came. We stayed there, holding one another for a while. He let his penis become flaccid within me, both enjoying each other's internal heat.

"I'm cold and sticky," I shuddered and giggled.

"Can we go down now?" he asked with arched eyebrows, humor in his eyes. We dressed one another and descended the stairs hand in hand.

22

I was startled to awake in James's arms. I remembered the night before and smiled. I kissed him, gently removed his arms from around my waist and got up. I was surprised to see that it was well after noon. I turned to watch James sleep wondering if I'd made a mistake. I couldn't be sure if I felt the same as he did. Yes, I had feelings for him but I wasn't in love with him and wasn't certain if I ever could be. The more I thought about it, the more I regretted what had happened.

"I don't want to hurt you," I whispered remorsefully staring at his slumbering form.

I jumped into the shower and began to wash my body as I let

my mind roam. It'd been a month since I'd bounced on Fabian and so much had changed. I was still hiding but James was doing a great job at keeping me distracted.

"I can't believe I slept with my best friend," I exclaimed aloud. I was so wrapped up in my reflections that I didn't hear the bathroom door open. I jumped and almost fell when I felt cold hands on my back. James steadied me while he laughed.

"You bastard!" I punched him in the gut.

"Mmmmm!" He moaned as he hugged me.

I stiffened under his touch. I didn't want him to delve too deeply into our tryst. We'd had a moment and that was all it was, at least for now. I just couldn't dwell on it, not until I got Fabian completely out of my world. I pulled away from James and got out of the bathroom.

"Why you runnin'?"

"I'm not runnin'. I'm just done showering, that's all." I dressed quickly hoping to be gone by the time he got out of the shower.

When I exited the room, James was just getting out of the shower. He planted an unreturned kiss on my lips. "What's wrong, ma?"

"Nothing," I pulled away and walked past him. I breathed deeply and turned to look at him. "Look, James, you deserve me to be honest with you. I'm just feeling claustrophobic right now and confused. I don't regret last night but ..."

"But what?" he asked hostilely as he walked toward me. I

stepped back frightened. James gasped. "India, I'm not Fabian. I would never lay a hand on you like that. Don't be scared of me."

Tears streaked my face. "I still got that nigga under my skin, James, and it isn't fair to either of us. I can't think about us, if there'll ever be an us until I'm out of this predicament. I'm sorry."

James shook his head, "I know, India. I can't help how I feel but I understand. I'm here for you regardless."

"I know. I just need to get away for a little while to think. I need to do something. I can't bear to look at these walls for another minute."

"Aight, where do you wanna go? Hold up, let me get dressed."

"No. I have to go alone, James. I need to be alone right now."

James's face fell. He looked at me, his nostrils flaring. I thought he was going to protest but instead he walked to his room and closed the door behind him. I grabbed my rollerblades and walked out before he could change his mind.

23

I put my rollerblades on in the lobby. I'd been fiending to jump on my wheels and escape everything and everyone. I wasn't sure if it was smart to go out on my own but I had to. I just needed to be alone. I knew I still had to be cautious and should stay in a well populated area. I decided to hit Central Park. As I bladed down Morningside Avenue, I savored the feeling of the rush of wind through my hair. For the first time in weeks, I felt like I was free and not trying to escape my past.

I entered Central Park at 110th Street. I got onto Park Drive and traversed the park quickly. This was the first time I'd rollerbladed since last summer. I'd been itching to blade but had been scared to go out roaming on my own. I didn't care anymore. At the moment, I was in the zone, meditating while I swung my body forward.

After going around the loop once, I exited on 59th Street and headed downtown. I negotiated the traffic easily. Staring at the lights of Times Square, I felt like a tourist, it'd been so long since I'd been south of 114th Street. I hit Chelsea Piers and checked out the flamboyant gay scene of NYC.

"Damn, I love this city!" I screamed. The queens stared at me strangely. I bladed along the West Side Highway and entered Battery Park City and didn't stop until I reached my spot, Purple Lights, a little pier protruding into the water at the southern edge of Manhattan, just north of Battery Park. I sat down, pulled out a joint and my journal. I wrote while I puffed, taking deep totes of the putrid smelling greens.

"Smells good," said a scraggly white guy that was walking by.

"Want the rest ?" I offered generously. I passed him the half smoked joint, put my back pack on and rolled away.

"Thanks, dude," he yelled after me.

I roamed southern Manhattan, taking my time now. I rolled through Wall Street, staring at the men in suits. God, I love a man in a suit, I thought to myself. So clean and classy.

I became annoyed with the increasing number of people on the streets and looked at my watch. Duh, it was rush hour. It was 5:30 pm so everyone was heading home. I felt SoHo beckoning me and turned north thinking I should start heading back. Ignoring my instincts, I roamed the streets of SoHo window shopping. By the time I realized, the sun was low over the Jersey skyline. "Damn, it'll be dark soon. I should head back."

I started rollerblading uptown, taking the side streets so as to avoid the jammed major arteries. I took out my cell and dialed James. "I'm on my way back."

He stood silent on the line momentarily. "I was worried. You can't bounce like that for hours without calling me. Not until this shit is over."

"I know. I'm sorry. I just needed…"

"To get away. Yeah, so you said …" He sounded upset. "Did you eat? Do you need anything?"

"No, I'll pick something up on the way. You want a slice from Koronet?" I asked, extending an olive branch.

"Sounds good. I'll see you when you get here. How long will you be?"

"I don't know. Another hour or so."

"I'll see you then."

"I love you, James, and I'm sorry."

"Yeah, me too. I'll see you when you get here."

He seemed calm now. I was relieved when I hung up; at least he wouldn't be fuming when I arrived. I didn't want to face that after having such a great day.

It was dark by the time I reached Riverside Drive. I was so focused on getting home that I didn't hear or see the black Range

Rover pulling up alongside me. When I finally became aware, it was too late. The backdoor flew open and a well-built arm reached out and grabbed me. I tried to scream, to fight but fell silent and blacked out when I unwillingly took a deep inhale of the noxious fumes coming from the handkerchief being held over my face.

24

I woke with a start. I'd dreamt again that Fabian had found me. Shivering violently, I tried to get up but couldn't. I looked up and saw that my wrists were tightly knotted to a bedpost with strips of white fabric. My eyes widened and I tried to scream but my desperate shouts were muffled by the gag in my mouth. My heart pounded in my chest as I tried to twist my body free only to discover that my legs were bound as well, splayed open. I was naked. I began to cry heaving sobs. My body shook fiercely. My worst nightmare had become a reality.

"Shut the fuck up!" I heard Fabian's hateful voice from the other side of the room.

I heard his footsteps approach the bed and trembled at the sight of his face, twisted in rage and disgust. "Oh, poor baby. What's wrong? You scared?" He backhanded me across the face, I saw stars. "Now you gotta pay the piper, you fuckin' whore! *¡Maldita sucia!*"

He mounted me. I tried to defend myself but resistance was futile. The combination of his weight and the shackles rendered me powerless against him. Fabian slapped me several times, making my head pound and nose bleed. I felt the cloth in my mouth moisten with my blood. Fabian glared at me laughing sinisterly. He punched me in the stomach and grabbed my breasts in his fists, twisting them while I writhed and moaned in agony.

"Where's my fuckin' money, you fuckin' dyke! ¡Traicionera! After everything I've done for you, this is how you gonna do me?!" He let go of my breasts and punched me across the temple. I passed out.

25

I was dragged into consciousness by a burning sensation in my pussy. I opened my eyes and smelled Fabian's rancid breath on my face.

"I was hoping you'd wake up," he whispered evilly in my ear. I screamed inaudibly as he thrust into me.

God, no! I prayed as he plunged into me brutally. I clenched my pelvic muscles hoping to drive him out but it only made him fuck me harder, sending searing spasms up my torso. Fabian bit my nipple viciously. I clamped my eyelids shut trying to block out the reality of what was happening to me - the man that I'd loved fiercely for five years of my life was now raping and torturing me.

"Open your eyes, *sucia,*" he yelled smacking me twice. I opened my swollen eyes and glared at him. I watched him while he assaulted me, cringing at the look of contempt on his grill. He clawed my body, pumping savagely, laughing at the tears rolling like rivers from my eyes. "Payback is a bitch!"

I recoiled with disgust when I felt his body stiffen in orgasm. Fabian wiped his dick and smeared his sperm on my face. He dismounted and spat in my face. "Dirty bitch!"

I cried quietly, my entire body heaved as I wept in desperation. I thought of James, 'Where are you? Help me please.' I wished I'd listened to him. If I'd paid attention to his concerns, I wouldn't be in this heinous predicament. For the first time in over a month, I prayed.

God, why have you forsaken me? Am I that evil a person? Do I not deserve your protection? Ay Dios, por favor! I made a mistake. A stupid mistake! No matter what, I do not deserve this. I have never been a malicious person, never intentionally hurt anyone … only Fabian … I wanted him to feel what I felt so I went and did something very stupid. I didn't think it through God … I know I deserve to be punished for my stupidity but this is too much. ¡Dios por favor, ayudame!

Fabian smacked me out of my prayer. "Cry, bitch! Cry! Nothing can compare to the tears I cried when I found out what you did. It's not even about the money. I got ten times that amount in the street. You of all people know that." I was shocked to see tears rolling down his face. "You left me, India. You just walked out on me and shacked up with that pussy nigga, James. What'd you think, I wouldn't find out?" He punched me twice in the ribs. I winced and coughed as I felt a rib crack. "You don't know me by now, India? You thought you were just gonna get away with it? Thought you were gonna live happily ever after with that *pallazo*? Thought you'd spend my money with that faggot? Huh?" He smacked me hard making blood pour out of my nose. "Why, India, why?" he bawled. "Why'd you do it? For the money? I would have given you that and more? Or is it that he fucked you better than me?"

I shook my head vehemently.

"No? Oh, so it's not true? You weren't fuckin' him? You gonna sit there and lie to me and tell me you didn't fuck that wack ass nigga?" His eyes were filled with a loathing I'd never seen. It frightened me to my core. "So I'm lying?!"

He stormed across the room and returned with my journal. My eyes widened with despair. I squirmed, trying uselessly to get loose. I shrank into myself as he read my private thoughts.

Date - April 15: I slept with James last night. I can't believe I slept with my best friend. I can't express the way it felt. For the first time in a long time, I felt loved, special. The way he held me, the way he ate me out … Ooooooh …

Fabian threw the book at my head. It struck me on the forehead and opened a nasty gash. I felt the blood trickle down into my matted hair. Fabian jumped on top of me and wrapped his hands around my throat. I gagged, struggling for air. My eyes bulged as I looked at him pleadingly. He glared at me fixedly, snot running out of his nose, his mouth distorted into a malicious sneer. Suddenly I felt my body slacken. So this is it, I thought. This is how it's going to happen ... how I am going to die.

Fabian let me go at once. His face softened and eyes filled with fear as he saw me coughing harshly, gasping for breath. He removed the gag to aid me and watched worriedly as I turned from blue to red. When I'd caught my breath, the sneer returned to his lips.

"You ain't getting off that easy, bitch! By the time I'm done with you, you're gonna wish you were dead." He punched me twice more in the stomach and the head. I faked unconsciousness. I knew only that would end this onslaught.

26

I kept my eyes shut praying that he'd leave. After a short time, God finally answered my prayers. I heard Fabian's heavy footsteps as they retreated. A door slammed and a lock bolted. I opened my eyes slowly after waiting a minute or two. My left eye was almost swollen shut but I could just make out the images around me. From the dank smell of the room and the low cinderblock ceiling, I could tell I was in a basement.

"I have to get out of here," I whispered through my cracked and swollen lips, realizing abruptly that Fabian hadn't put the gag back on. I heaved a sigh and winced at the piercing pain that pounded my side. I was certain that I had a cracked rib, if not more. My entire body ached but I forced my attention away from the agony. I had to get out of there. There was no time to wallow in my sorrow or assess my injuries. I had to get out!

I looked up at my bindings and noticed that though I was still shackled, my left wrist had loosened during the struggle with Fabian. I pulled on my arm slightly ignoring the sting from my raw flesh rubbing against the rough fabric. I had to check the tightness of the knot and try to figure out how it had loosened. When I pulled, I saw that the knot was weak. The more I pulled, the looser it became. My heart rate accelerated when I saw that I almost had it. When I heard what sounded like footsteps I abandoned my efforts. I couldn't let my tormentor see that I had almost freed myself. He'd just retie me even tighter, and I'd have to start from scratch. I didn't think he intended on letting me live that long.

I again feigned unconsciousness when Fabian walked into the room. He walked over to me and brushed my hair aside in a seemingly loving manner. I recoiled and shot my eyes open when I felt a damp cloth against my face. I was shocked to find that he was wiping my face off. Without saying a word, Fabian cleaned the blood off my face and tended to my wounds.

"Sshhh." He silenced me softly when I whimpered as he cleaned my injuries with alcohol. When he was done, he gave me some water to drink and asked if I was hungry. I shook my head and turned my face away. I was confused by his actions but hadn't this always been Fabian? Cruel one moment and tender the next. I became angry at myself when I felt the tears well up in my eyes. There's no time for this India, I lectured.

Suddenly, Fabian was on me again. I felt the cold steel of a gun against my temple and recognized the murderous look in his eyes. I was terrified, no doubt, but somehow felt that he was not going to kill me, at least not this way.

"Look at me, bitch," Fabian muttered through clenched teeth. I looked at Fabian trying to think of what to say.

"Is this what you want? To see me battered and broken? To have me at your mercy? Well, you got it." I let the tears flow from my eyes freely.

"Oh, now I'm supposed to feel bad for you?" He dug the gun into my temple. I cried out feebly. "Well, I don't feel bad. I don't feel shit for you anymore, you fuckin' ho!" He gritted his teeth but his eyes betrayed him. I could see that he still loved me. Beneath his resentment and malevolence, I still held a space in his heart. I had to take advantage of this weakness.

"I loved you, Fabian. Loved you like I've never loved before and will never love again." I cried as I felt the firearm cut into my skin. "You think you're the only one that's hurting?" I began to howl as I thought about our tumultuous relationship. "No one's ever hurt me the way you have!"

I was relieved when Fabian removed the gun from my brow. He fell on my chest sobbing. I let him cry and faked concern. "I'm sorry, pa. I'm sorry I abandoned you but… I was just so brokenhearted

... I ... I couldn't take it ... I had to run away ..." Fabian looked at me. My heart pounded hoping he bought my insincere apologies. "Please, baby. Forgive me. Please ... let me go ... Please ..."

Fabian sat back on the bed and let his eyes scan my body. I wished I could read his mind. "So now that I got you like this, you want me to forgive you, right? I'm supposed to believe that you still love me, right?" Before I could deceptively proclaim my love, he jumped on me and started pistol whipping me. I bellowed in sheer anguish and excruciating pain. I felt my bones shatter beneath the weight of the gun. Mercifully, I blacked out.

The pounding in my head eventually brought me back to reality. My left eye was now swollen shut and I could barely keep the right one open due to the agonizing ache in my head. But I knew that I didn't have the luxury of considering my wounmds. I was certain that if I did not get out now, I would die at the hands of my first love. I remained still and silent for a while to ensure that I was alone in the room before I went to work on the knot again. When I was certain, I began pulling at my arm disregarding the cramping in my body. I whimpered quietly when my arm came loose. "Oh God, please. Help me get out of here." The salty tears stung my bruised face.

I used my free hand to unravel the knot that bound my right wrist. When I tried to raise my body to untie the fetters on my ankles,

I screeched in pain. The loud noise startled me and I lay back down, fearful that Fabian would hear and return to rebind me and sadistically strike me again. I held my breath nervously as I listened for a sound but heard only silence. Slowly, I raised my battered body. I held my side with one hand and freed myself with the other.

Before getting out of the bed, I scanned the room for any signs of exit. I'd heard Fabian lock the door behind him earlier so I knew that probably wasn't an option. I got up and tried the door anyway only to find that my suspicions were correct – the door was bolted shut. In the far left hand corner of the room, over a disheveled couch, I saw a small window. I limped over to it and determined that with effort I could fit my body through but first I had to find something to break the window with. I knew that as soon as I shattered the glass, I would have to hurry out because Fabian was certain to hear the crash.

I searched the room and found the pail with bloody water that Fabian used to clean my wounds. I emptied the water, climbed atop the couch and practiced my intended movements. I didn't bother to consider that I was naked, that I didn't know where I was or where I was going. My only thought was getting out of there fast.

I dug up all the strength that was left in my body and with one hard motion, smashed the window with the pail. I used the bed sheet to quickly wipe the glass from the sill and tried to pull myself through the tiny crevice. I hadn't thought about the strength it would take to heave my body up through the window. On my first attempt, my battered body failed me and I almost fell back onto the floor. I quickly collected myself and tried again, this time putting most of my weight on my right side where my ribs were still intact. With difficulty, I pulled myself through.

When I saw the star ridden night sky, I began to moan in relief but stopped myself. "There's no time for that, India. You have to get the fuck out of here!" I ran as fast as I could, scanning my surroundings as I ran. I was in a wooded area. From the position of the moon and the bitter cold of the air, I could tell that it was the middle of the night, maybe two or three a.m. I was so high on adrenaline that I barely felt the shrubs scratch my bare legs, arms and torso as I ran.

"Where do I go, God? Please! Give me a sign," I pleaded as I looked around desperately.

Suddenly, I heard a rustle to my right and stopped dead in my tracks. I stood motionless, listened and watched. To my amazed eyes, a young deer emerged through the bushes. My eyes almost popped out of my head.

"This must be the sign!" I thought aloud and ran in the direction from where it appeared.

I ran for what seemed like years. My legs and feet were bloody with cuts and scrapes, my body mangled but I pushed on. "I am not going to die here!" I told myself repeatedly. Soon I saw a light in the distance and began to run faster in that direction. I came upon a country road, looked in both directions but saw nothing, no approaching cars, no pedestrians.

"Where should I go, God? Which direction?" I beseeched the heavens. I heard an owl hoot to my left and went in that direction. I could no longer run, my energy was depleting quickly. I limped along, hoping to find a phone, for a car to pass, something or someone to save me. After walking for a while, my body finally yielded. I collapsed onto the road. I tried to pull herself up but couldn't. I couldn't even crawl. My body had been pushed to its limit. It began to break down as I lay there wailing, praying for a miracle.

27

I thought I'd died when I saw lights twinkling in the distance. So it's true what they say. This is how it is when you die? You start seeing light in the distance and shit ... I chuckled at the cruelty of it all and grimaced at the consequent pain. I saw the lights getting closer and my fading hope rekindled. As the lights grew larger and brighter, I realized that it was not a hallucination. There was really a car coming towards me.

All I need is for this guy to not see me and run over me. I sniggered at how ironic that would be and regretted it immediately as spasms of pain pulsed throughout my body. I have to pick up my arm to try to signal him but how? I breathed shallow breaths and waited until the car was closer. I gathered all my strength and shot my arm up, waving it from side to side twice before it caved in and crumpled to my side. Miraculously, it was enough. The car stopped in front of me and a woman stepped out.

"Oh my God, Dave. It's a woman! Oh Lord, what have they done to you? Ma'am, are you okay?" she asked as she picked up my head and cradled it on her lap. A man came running out of the vehicle and halted when he saw my naked bloody body lying in a heap on the pavement. "Come help me, Dave," screamed the lady frantically. "We have to take this poor girl to the hospital."

I groaned as they lifted me and walked slowly to the car. "Oh, God help her!" implored Dave as they put me in the backseat and covered me with a shawl. That was the last thing I heard before I fell unconscious.

28

I could hear people moving around me. I struggled to open my eyes and found that only my right eye would open just slightly. The bright overhead light made me squint uncomfortably. I tried to move my arm and became anguished when I saw that it was restrained.

"No!" I cried.

"She's in shock, doctor," said a female voice. "It's okay, ma'am," soothed the voice. "You're in the hospital. You're safe now. Can you tell me your name?"

I looked up at the blurry figure staring down at me. I blinked repeatedly in an effort to clear my vision. "India ..." I whispered with great exertion. "India Maldonado."

"What did she say?" asked another female voice. "Did she say India Maldonado? That's the missing girl from New York City. It's been all over the news."

"Did you say India Maldonado?" asked the first voice.

I nodded my head slightly and scowled at the stabbing soreness in my neck.

"Okay, ma'am. Yes, that's her name," said the first voice to the second. "Relax, don't move. We're gonna take care of you. You're going to be just fine."

I passed out before I could say or hear anything further.

I awoke to the vibrating hum and shallow beeping of machines. I opened my one good eye to see that I was in a stark white room. I could smell the stale disinfectant odor of hospital air. I could barely move my neck but with effort I was able to glance around. I saw a large bouquet of colorful flowers on the night table to the left of my bed - orchids and irises. "Beautiful," I whispered.

A nurse entered the room. "Oh, you're awake finally, Ms. Maldonado," she said smiling.

"Where am I?" I asked raspily.

The nurse put a cup of water to my lips. I gulped thirstily though it smarted my throat. "You're in Oswego Medical Center. You've been here five days, ma'am."

"Five days!" I exclaimed. "¡Dios mio, no!"

"It's okay, ma'am."

I immediately recognized her voice. "You attended to me when they brought me in, right?"

"Yes, I did. You were quite a sight but you're healing now. You're going to be fine."

"Thank you for taking care of me," I said in between sobs.

"Just doing my job, ma'am." But the nurse's eyes betrayed her. She'd grown fond of the patient in room 218.

"So, who is this James you've been crying for? You've called for him several times in your sleep."

I thought of James longingly. "I should have listened," I whispered. I was too wrapped up in my remorse to hear the door open.

"She's awake now. You can come in. She's going to be just fine."

I turned to see James walking towards me. It was like seeing an angel for the first time. We cried together as he held my hand and stared at my lumped up face.

"I should have listened," I whimpered.

Tears streaked down James's face in torrents. "I should have been more understanding. I'm sorry." He tried to hug me but pulled away quickly when he felt me flinch.

"Be careful now," said the nurse. "She's got two broken ribs, a fractured nose and severe contusions. It's going to take some time for her to heal so you have to handle her with care." The nurse injected my IV with medicine through a syringe. She patted me on the leg before walking out. "You're safe now, honey. No one's going to hurt you anymore."

I looked at James while he sniffled. "I thought you were dead. I should have taken better care of you, kept a closer eye on you. I slept and that motherfucker took advantage."

I was astonished to hear James blaming himself for what happened. If anyone was to blame, I was. I was the reckless one who had foolishly acted on impulse. I tried to console James but felt suddenly groggy as the medication took affect. I gazed into James's eyes until I floated off to sleep.

29

I heard a strange voice calling me in the distance and struggled to open my eyes. I couldn't understand why my left eye wouldn't open. I put my hand to my face and was instantly reminded of the brutal abduction and torture by the layers of bandages. I heard the voice again, calling my name. I opened my good eye slightly.

"Ms. Maldonado, I'm Detective Pierce and this is my partner Detective Morales. I know you've been through a lot and probably don't want to relive what happened to you but I have to ask you some questions that can help capture the man who did this to you."

I stared at the officer in dismay. What the fuck does he mean 'to help capture?' They haven't caught him yet?! I was startled out of my thoughts by the sound of a familiar voice and the comforting touch of a warm hand. I turned and saw my mother, Consuelo. The tears flowed unabated.

I hadn't spoken to my mother in over three years. She disapproved of my relationship with Fabian and made no secret of it. She'd lecture me constantly about the dangers of being involved with *un hombre de la calle*. We'd get into screaming matches that would usually end with me storming out and not talking to her for weeks.

One steaming summer day, I decided to rollerblade to my mom's crib in Brooklyn. I was so sweaty and uncomfortable by the time I arrived that I decided to take a shower. My mother walked in as I was drying myself off and saw the black and blues on my back. Being the protective mother that she was, she demanded I tell her who'd done that to me. I fabricated a story about falling down the stairs but Mom knew better. The next day, she went to the block and confronted Fabian. She smacked him across the face and threatened to kill him if he ever laid a hand on her child again. Fabian stood there in disbelief, too shocked to say or do anything. It was I who reacted angrily, pushing my mother away, cursing her, vowing that I would never speak to her again. "How dare you disrespect my husband?" I yelled repeatedly.

I'd kept my promise. My mother tried to reach out to me several times, sending me long, grief-stricken letters and leaving me sobbing messages, but I would not relent. I was too stupid in love to realize that my mother was only concerned for my welfare, despondent at the loss of her only child. I broke down as I recalled that day.

"I'm so sorry," I mouthed to my mother over and over.

"Sshhh," soothed Consuelo tearfully. "Just answer his questions. *Hablámos despues.*"

"Ma'am, I... I can only imagine how difficult this is for you," muttered Detective Morales.

"No... I'll tell you everything." I felt a sudden surge of strength. I was going to make sure that Fabian paid dearly for what he'd done to me. "The man who did this to me was the love of my life."

I squeezed my mother's hand as I recounted the nightmare that I had endured.

It didn't take long for the Oswego authorities to find the cabin where Fabian had held me captive. Although it had seemed much farther, I had only run two miles before being found. Still, despite their joint efforts with the NYC and Yonkers Police Departments, Fabian remained on the lam. Officials downstate searched his apartment on Tuckahoe Road, found the kilos of cocaine and even a large supply of heroine that I had known nothing about. They set up surveillance vans to spy his usual hangouts round the clock but when I was released two weeks after being rushed to the emergency room near death, Fabian still hadn't been detained.

I tried not to think of this frightening fact. I had to focus on my recovery. When I'd been brought into Oswego Medical Center, I was in shock and suffering from hypothermia, exposure, extreme exhaustion and dehydration. My lung had collapsed, I had two broken ribs and a fractured nose. The left side of my face was hideously bruised but thankfully it was just flesh wounds. When I left the hospital, my eye was still swollen shut but the doctors assured me that my vision would go back to normal after a few days of blurriness. To the doctor's surprise, I hadn't suffered any nerve damage either. When she saw a picture of me in the newspapers, my attending doctor told me, "I'm confident you'll be back to your gorgeous self in no time."

I had also unknowingly sprained my wrist when I'd pulled repeatedly on the tethers to free myself. In spite of my extensive injuries, I complained that the worst was a rip to my labia that occurred during the ferocious rape. The tear required over thirty stitches and whenever I had to urinate, the nurses could hear my screeches down the hall.

As James wheeled me out of the hospital in the wheelchair, I was surprised to see Professor Daines standing with my mother beside a police cruiser. I put my head down, ashamed of my ghastly bruises. Professor Daines kneeled next to me and put her finger under my chin. She smiled. "I've missed you. Class just isn't the same without your feisty criticisms."

I smiled half-heartedly. "I'm a mess," I whispered.

The professor tenderly cupped my black and blue face. "No you're not. You're just a little broken and we're all here to help you pick up the pieces."

Mom kissed me on the forehead. "I don't know if you're gonna like what we have to tell you."

They all looked at me concerned. "Nena, you know Fabian hasn't been found." James said finally. "So it's not safe for you to come home with me or to go to your Mom's crib."

I looked at the three of them with despair in my eyes. "Then where the hell am I gonna go?"

"The police thought it was best that you go into protective custody," Professor Daines informed me calmly.

"I don't wanna go with the cops. I already feel like I've been imprisoned for the past two months! I wanna go home." I began to sob loudly. "Mommy, please, take me home," I pleaded.

"*No puedo*, India. What if he comes to look for you there?" My mother held my head to her breast, comforting me.

"We knew you wouldn't agree to that, India," continued Professor Daines. "So I offered to let you stay with me in my home in the Poconos. The police thought it would be safe since Fabian... Is that his name?" she asked quickly before going on. "Fabian knows nothing about our relationship so there's no way he could know you're with me." I turned to look at my mentor. I couldn't believe her kindness. "The police are also concerned that Fabian will go after your mother and James to get to you so I've offered that they stay with me as well.

There'll be a patrol car outside the house 24/7, just in case but ..."

Before the professor could finish, I had thrown my arm around her neck. "Thank you, thank you," I repeated, tears of gratitude rolling down my face.

As we drove to Pennsylvania, a police escort in tow, I stared out the window. "What about school, Professor?"

"I've arranged with your professors to have your final assignments and exams e-mailed to you. You'll still be graduating on time, okay?" She winked and smiled at me in the rear view mirror.

I was still having trouble swallowing all that had happened to me in the short span of six weeks. You won't get the best of me, I thought to myself silently.

30

The sun sparkled off the calm waters of Lake Towamensing. I sat on a chair by the shore, watching the ripple of the water on the lake's edge and listening to the harmonious sounds of nature. I was relieved to be away from the city, far from everything that had caused me grief. Still, a part of me was sullen. I'd waited so anxiously for the day that I would don the baby blue gown with the Columbia crown stitched neatly on the lapel and the cap with the gold tassel swinging to the side. I'd dreamt of walking across the stage and receiving my degree, gushing with pride and accomplishment. But Fabian had dashed yet another one of my dreams. There was absolutely no way I could attend commencement while Fabian was still on the street.

I turned to see a woodpecker drilling a hole in a tree. I watched curiously as the bird chiseled away at the wood. I was so engrossed in watching the bird toil that I didn't see James walk up and sit on the grass next to me.

"How you feeling?"

I sighed and without looking responded, "This shit sucks, James. We can't even go to our own graduation because of this dick. I'm sorry I dragged you into this. If I hadn't, you'd be home, safe from harm." I stared at the blue black water blankly as the afternoon shadows lengthened across the expanse.

"That's bullshit, India. I got involved willingly. You didn't make me do shit."

I looked at James sadly. Our first night there, James had tried to climb into bed with me. Just the presence of a man in my bed nauseated me. I couldn't help how I felt and didn't know how to tell James. When he tried to hold me, I cowered and balled myself into fetal position at the opposite side of the bed. Moments later, I felt James climb out of the bed. The following morning, I found him sleeping on the couch. We hadn't discussed or even mentioned it at all since. I had immersed myself in completing my final requirements, using it as an excuse to avoid James altogether.

"Look James, I... I'm sorry I've been so distant. I just..." I stuttered.

"You don't have to explain. I can only imagine what you're going through. I understand that you can't handle this or us right now. I'll wait as long as I have to," he said sincerely.

I didn't know how to tell him that I didn't know if there would ever be an 'us'. Right then, I couldn't fathom being intimate with any man. That was just the farthest thing from my mind. James rose and walked back towards the house. I felt bad but I was honestly relieved that he'd left. I had other more important things to think about.

I looked down at the laptop on the table beside me. In the week and a half I'd been in the Pocono Mountains, I'd completed all my requirements, taken my finals and written my papers except for this last one. It was Professor Daines's final. While it appeared simple at first sight, I couldn't bring myself to begin. I didn't know in what direction to take it. I reread the assignment for what must have been the tenth time.

Write a fictional biography, in first person, of up to 1500 words. There are no boundaries; you can decide to be flamboyant or conservative in creating the fictional person. Be sure to remain in touch with the process of writing. Consider the inspiration for the piece – your aspirations, the lives of others, etc. And, finally, be conscious of how your imagination is working. Good luck!

Ideas soared through my mind. I picked up the laptop, placed it on my lap and stared at the hauntingly blank screen. "Fuck!" I muttered in frustration. I found it impossible to make sense of the jumble of thoughts that inundated my skull.

"India," interrupted my mother. "*Ven a comer, m'ija.* I made your favorite. *Sopa de frijoles* with boiled green bananas and white rice."

My mouth salivated. I put the laptop down roughly. "Maybe some food will help me focus." I ambled to the house slowly, deeply inhaling the crisp, unpolluted air as I walked. I stopped to sniff the roses in Professor Daines's garden, hissing when I pricked myself on a thorn.

"I wonder where he is now," I pondered grudgingly.

Sitting at the table, I watched my mother move around the kitchen methodically. She hasn't changed at all, I thought as she poured a large bowl of soup thick with vegetables and meat. Mom hadn't let me do anything since we'd arrived. She woke early to prepare breakfast for everyone and when the clock struck noon, she stopped whatever she was doing to prepare lunch ensuring that each meal consisted of one of my favorite recipes. She spent the day cleaning, cooking and tending to my healing, dressing my wounds and giving me my prescribed medications.

Pangs of guilt smarted me as I gazed at my mother's plump figure approaching me with a tray of food. I stared into my mother's eyes, looking for any signs of resentment or rancor and found none.

Mom kissed my healing face and instructed, "*Te comes todo, sabés."* She caressed me lovingly, "Your bruises have healed nicely. Look, you can open your eye again and your *morados* are fading."

She blinked back tears and turned away quickly. She walked to the sink and started to wash dishes. I saw that my mother's shoulders were quivering slightly. She was crying again. On several occasions, I'd overheard my mother's muffled sobs through the door to her room but whenever I tried to enter to console her, I found the door locked. When Mom came to the door, her eyes were puffy.

"Estas loca. My eyes are red because I was napping. *Estoy vieja ya.* I need more sleep these days," she'd say with a contrived chuckle.

I rose from my chair, walked over and put my arms around my mother's broad waist. I put my face on her shoulder and drew in a deep breath. I recognized the scent that soothed me when I was just a child, a surprisingly compatible combination of rich Latin spices and Oscar De La Renta, Mom's favorite perfume.

"Que pasa, m'ija?" Mom asked as she soaped the dishes with quaking hands.

"You're crying again." My voice cracked.

"Estoy bien. Go eat. You need the nutrients. It will help you get strong." She shrugged her shoulders and nudged me away.

I walked back to the table and stared at the steaming bowl of soup. It smelled delicious but I couldn't get myself to taste a morsel. I bit my lip, fighting the tears gathering in the corners of my eyes.

I thought back to my childhood and the many times my

mother had prepared this very meal. Whenever I was sick or feeling down, Mom toiled away in the kitchen cooking her soup, knowing that it would rid me of whatever illness was plaguing me. It was my elixir, a seemingly mystical potion with the power to heat my insides and obliterate all pains and sorrows.

"*¿Que te pasa?*" Mom asked putting her hand on my head. "Why haven't you tasted the soup? Don't you want it?"

"I don't deserve this, Ma," I said. I buried my face in my hands shamefully.

"Don't be silly, *m'ija*. You deserve that and more."

I stared at my mother with incredulity. "How can you say that after how I've treated you? I turned my back on you for a *mierda* of a man. You tried to tell me, to show me that he was *basura* but I wouldn't listen."

"*¿De que hablas?* You still stuck on the past?" Mom kneeled beside me. "You are a different person now. I didn't know you then. You didn't even know yourself. I've forgiven you, *hija*. Now you have to forgive yourself. Only then will you be able to move on." She hugged me, stood up, grabbed the spoonful of broth and shoved it into my mouth.

I giggled playfully and savored the food. "Mmmmm, *sopita*." I opened my mouth for another spoon. Mom fed me as she had when I was just a toddler. After several spoonfuls, I took the spoon from her mother's hand. "Okay, Ma, *ya*! I feel like I'm two again," I said laughing and put a piece of green banana in my mouth.

Consuelo snickered. *"Buen provecho."* She walked back to the sink and continued to clean.

Only a mother loves so unconditionally, I thought as I feasted on my favorite dish.

31

I walked around Professor Daines's house hunting for James. I peered into each of the six bedrooms, the three bathrooms and the basement turned playroom but came up empty. I checked the front and back gardens, was greeted by the chirping of crickets, hooting of owls and the lulling sounds of other nocturnal creatures, but found no James. Where can he be?

I made my way to the edge of the lake and sat at my usual spot. I stared at the reflection of the crescent moon on the water and shivered as a breeze went up the back of my t-shirt. I jumped when I heard a ruffle of leaves and stood up readying to defend myself if need be. Professor Daines's waifish figure came through the bushes.

She had her hands up as if in surrender.

"Relax. It's just me, India."

I sighed. "I hate this, Professor Daines. I can't hear a branch crack without getting frightened."

"It'll be over soon," Professor Daines said reassuringly. "And, please do me a favor, call me Joanna. We're not in the classroom and have developed a deeper relationship than that of professor and student." We both smiled and looked out at the water.

"It's beautiful here. I hope to have a house like this one day."

"This is my little escape. When I need to get away from the hustle and bustle of city life, I come here, disconnect my phone and bond with nature. It's quite refreshing." She looked at me and with twinkling eyes said, "And I'm certain you will have this and more."

"I hope so," I responded, a hint of envy in my voice.

"So, I sent all of your final exams and papers to your professors. They're all happy to hear you're getting better and are safe. Professor Thurman, your Indo-Tibetan Buddhism professor, says he misses you. He informed me that you are quite the Buddhist in training." She laughed and jabbed me in the ribs playfully. "Sorry!" she cried apologetically when I winced.

"It's okay. They don't hurt as bad anymore. I can actually get out of bed without wanting to scream in pain."

"I couldn't help but notice that you have just one final left to complete. Mine." Joanna looked at me inquisitively.

I grinned guiltily at my mentor. "It's not that I haven't tried, I just... I guess I have writer's block. My other assignments were different. They didn't require imagination. Yours does and I just haven't managed to get my juices churning."

"India, stop thinking about it so much. Just do it. Just write. Don't over-analyze it. Act like you're writing in your journal. Let it be a flow of consciousness but with a specific subject matter in mind." Joanna arched her eyebrows, winked at me and started walking up to the house.

"Hey, professor," I called. "Have you seen James?"

"He went for a walk, I think. He has a lot on his plate too, you know."

I watched Joanna's thin frame disappear into the house. I thought of James and how he must be feeling. He was in love with me while I was suffering from a broken heart and battered soul. I couldn't think about him and his needs while all he could think about was me and my needs.

"I'd still rather be him than me right now," I mused.

It was well past two in the morning but I still hadn't managed to drift off to sleep. I tossed and turned in the bed until, frustrated, I decided to get up. As I passed the living room, I saw James sprawled on the couch. I walked toward his sleeping figure and was overcome by the reeking odor of alcohol, Hennessy to be exact.

"Ugh," I moaned. I shook my head and turned to walk away but stopped when I looked down and saw something peeking out of James's jacket. I reached down and was elated to find it was a tightly rolled joint. "Heaven! I'm in heaven," I sang.

I grabbed a sweater from my room then walked to my chair by the lake's edge. I lit the joint, took deep drags of the fetid smelling grass and giggled at how quickly the euphoric effects hit me. "Damn, it's been a minute, huh?" I had to turn the joint off after smoking only half because I was so high. I stared out at the twinkle of lights in the houses across the lake. I shifted my attention to the laptop still sitting on the table beside me. Hmmmm, I thought. I should take a stab at Professor D's final now that I'm high. Some of my best shit was written under the influence. Fuck it, why not?!

I picked up the laptop, turned it on and tapped my chipped nails on the keys as I waited for it to load. I opened Microsoft Word and looked apprehensively at the blank page. Don't think, just write! I ignored the ache in my wrist as I started typing.

My name is Anais Rodriguez. A moment ago I learned that I am this year's winner of the coveted National Book Award for Fiction for my latest novel, In the Wake of the Storm. In addition, several days ago I was asked to speak at my Alma Mater's commencement and am astonished at my good fortune. Two years ago, I won the National Book Award for Non Fiction for my memoir, Soul of the Bumblebee. This was my first published work and

I never in my life imagined that it would receive such accolades. And, now, my novel has received national acclaim as well …

"My cup runneth over." Those were my exact words when the reporters asked for my reaction at hearing of my second award. I made it a point to thank my husband Ruben for his unwavering support and daughter Aria for her unrelenting inspiration.

My daughter is a miracle child. After four miscarriages, I had resigned myself to the possibility that I'd never bear fruit from my womb. The doctors told me that I had "an inhospitable uterus," whatever that means. Ruben and I thought of adopting but I became so depressed at the thought that we decided to put off the idea for a while. It's not that I never wanted to adopt. I just always thought I'd do so after having a child of my own. During a routine "woman check-up" my doctor asked me if I thought I might be pregnant. Naturally, I told her there was absolutely no way. She gave me a pregnancy test regardless and to my surprise, I was with child.

My husband and I were cautiously ecstatic. It may seem like an oxymoron but it's the truth. We were overjoyed at the possibility of finally having a child but were wary not to get too excited since we'd already experienced the heart wrenching tragedy of losing a number of babies. I was put on immediate bed rest. It was during those months that I wrote my first novel. Thank God, both my child and my book brightened my world several months later.

I never imagined I could be a stay-at-home mom but when Aria came into the world, I could not fathom leaving her. Perhaps it was the fact that I'd tried so many times before but just the thought of leaving her in the care of someone else sent me into hysterical crying fits. My husband was hesitant at first, after all we had a mortgage to pay and other mounting bills. I convinced him that this was the best thing for both Aria and me, and told him that perhaps now I could actually concentrate on my dream of becoming a writer.

Watching Aria grow, going from breastfeeding to bottle feeding, sleeping through the night for the first time, taking her first steps and finally becoming potty trained after several breakdowns on my part and fits of rage on hers, inspired me to write the first of what I hope to be a pentagonía of memoirs.

I must also thank my mother for her inspiration in the form of stories about her motherland, Honduras, and the obstacles she overcame to give us a better life. My mother constantly reminded me that life is nothing if one does not follow one's calling. From her I learned that one's past is one's foundation but should never be one's demise for while it is a part of us and makes us who we are, it does not determine our destiny nor who we will eventually become.

Without my daughter, my mother and my husband, I don't believe I would be who I am. I wouldn't have followed my heart's desire and become the award-winning writer that I now am ... They are the subject of my commencement speech.

I was shocked at how much had come out of me. "Damn, Professor D was right. I just had to write and not think about it." I put the laptop down and walked back to the house. I finally felt like I could get some sleep.

32

I was snatched from my slumber by my mother and Joanna jumping on my bed like small children.

"What the hell is wrong with you people?" I yelled half annoyed and half amused. James walked in the room with a tray of breakfast.

"Someone deserves breakfast in bed," he said with a Kool-Aid smile pasted on his hung over looking face.

"What's going on?" I asked, looking at everyone suspiciously.

"We wanted to give you the news together over a nice breakfast of bagels and coffee," Professor Daines teased, grabbing a cinnamon raisin bagel and taking a huge bite of it.

"What news? What are you guys scheming?"

"No one is scheming anything, *m'ija,*" said Mom, shaking her head and pursing her lips playfully.

"You guys are killing me! What's going on?" I demanded anxiously.

"Well…" Mom looked at her two conspirators giggling. "The cops found Fabian hiding out in DR. He's being extradited back to the U.S. as we speak!"

"Shut up!" I exclaimed. I lurched out of bed in one leap and stared at my mother, James and Joanna. "Y'all are shitting me! This is some serious shit, y'all! You can't play with me like this. Tell me you're not joking!"

"We wouldn't play with your emotions like that, India," James said beaming.

I threw my arms around his neck and planted a kiss on his lips. Then I jumped on the bed and started jumping up and down. I felt like I was ten again and had just found out that Mom had bought me the popular Strawberry Shortcake bike.

"*¡Gracias a Dios!*" I screamed at the top of my lungs and threw my arms around my mother, almost knocking her down. I then turned and embraced my mentor, knocking the wind out of her. Suddenly I stopped and fell onto the bed in sobs. "I know I shouldn't be crying. I should be happy but… I feel like I'm finally free and…"

"*Esta bien, m'ija,* we understand," soothed my mother, holding me close and crying with me. "We're all free now."

Professor D kneeled in front of me. "So, commencement is in a couple of days. Looks like you're going to have your dream after all."

"I hadn't even thought about that. We're going to commencement? We're going to commencement!" I sang as I skipped around James. "I told you that you wouldn't get the best of me," I mused, overjoyed at the latest development of my saga.

33

I walked out into the warm morning air, took a long, deep breath and whispered, "This is the beginning of your new life India." I walked down the path towards the lake and stopped dead when I saw Professor D absorbed intently at something she was reading on my laptop.

"Hey, what are you doing?" I asked lightheartedly.

"Just reading something a student of mine wrote," Joanna hovered over the laptop chuckling.

"You're reading what I wrote? Professor Deeeeeee," I whined. "That's the first draft. You're not supposed to read it yet. Let me get that." I tried to snatch the computer.

"No, no, no! You're done writing. I don't need you to edit or rewrite or anything. This is exactly what I wanted from you, a flow of consciousness. I'm giving you an A on your final and for the semester." She extended her hand for me to shake. "Congratulations, you are now officially a graduate of Columbia University."

I let go of Joanna's hand and embraced her tightly. "If it wasn't for you ..."

"Save it, India! I know how grateful you are. The truth is that you are the daughter I never had. We're both blessed to have each other." She smiled at me devotedly. "Now, tell me, what were your inspirations? I'm dying of curiosity."

Joanna passed me the laptop. I quickly read what I'd typed the night before while in my marijuana induced stupor. I was astonished by the names I'd unconsciously given the characters. What ever happened to Anais, I wondered. And Ruben? How odd I gave that name to the husband in my story.

"Well, I guess Anais is who I wish I was. Who I hope to become - a resilient, accomplished, driven woman. Ruben is the perfect husband I hope to find, supportive, loving, understanding. And my mother, well, that's self-explanatory. You see how she is with me in spite of what I've put her through. Aria is the daughter I hope to have one day."

"Then you know where to start. This is the first day of your life. Get to work. You have a novel and your memoirs to write!" Joanna made a silly face and laughed.

I sat down, put the computer on my lap and started typing away. If not now, when? I reflected as my fingers danced across the keyboard.

34

I beamed as I stared at myself in the mirror. "I make this cap and gown look good." I giggled and turned to model for my mother.

Mom's eyes moistened. "See *m'ija,* when you have faith, things work themselves out." She kissed me and adjusted my cap.

I walked into the living room of James's suite and struck a pose. "You really do make that ugly thing look good." He laughed. We then impatiently took a million and one pictures for our families.

"C'mon, let's go, please," I insisted with a tinge of annoyance. We walked together towards the South Lawn.

"Damn, James, four years flew by fast, huh?"

"It's amazing, isn't it? Our college careers are officially over."

I stood on College Walk staring at my graduating class as they bustled about, passing bottles of champagne, smoking cigars and cheering their accomplishment. I unzipped my gown a little and discreetly pulled a blunt from my cleavage. "We can't graduate without celebrating with an L." I flaunted my nicely rolled L, passing it under James's nose.

"Mmm, it's the good shit too!"

"Northern lights, baby! This shit costs $400 for a half an ounce but it's worth every penny." I took a deep whiff of the *grajo* smelling ganja. "Let's go find a seat." I led us toward the middle of the crowd.

As soon as the President of the University began his longwinded speech, I lit the L. "Here's to the beginning of the rest of our lives." We gave each other high fives and ciphered the L.

"Damn, that shit smells incredible," I heard someone say behind me. I turned to see a preppie white dude smiling hopefully at me. His face dropped when he saw the bruises on my face. I'd tried to hide them the best I could with makeup but the darkest ones around my eye and the left side of my face were still visible, more so in the mid-morning sun.

"Want some?" I asked, ignoring the dude's reaction. I passed him the blunt. "Congrats!"

The prep passed me a glass of champagne, "Cristal, baby! Enjoy and congrats to you as well."

As the ganja-induced bliss penetrated, I thought about the

events of the past few weeks. Who thought I'd be sitting here after all that craziness?

"I'm finally fuckin' free!" I said too loud. "Oops," I giggled as several graduates turned to look at me with big grins.

When my name was called, I walked onto the stage proudly. I still was in awe of myself. As I shook the president's hand, I took off my cap and flashed it to the crowd. FREEDOM! was sprawled across the top. The president smirked and the crowd broke into stomach clutching laughter as I one hand cart wheeled my way off the stage.

35

I sipped my drink as I stared around the crowded room. These people are crazy! I thought. Mom, Professor D and James had surprised me with a graduation party. I turned to look at James who was ogling me with a big grin on his face.

"Surprised?"

"Surprised isn't the word! But this is your day too, pa."

"Nah, this is all about you babe," James leaned over to kiss me on the forehead. "Oh, you look stunning in that dress by the way." He stared at me up and down and nodded his head approvingly.

"Oh, this old thing," This dress is off the hook, I thought looking down at myself. It was a low cut, plum colored Dior dress. I had initially wanted to buy a short Versace dress I'd seen in a magazine but my legs were still scratched up from my run in the woods. I fell in love with the Dior dress as soon as I saw it in the store. The long sleeve dress had a plunging neckline that stopped right below my breasts, was fitted around my torso and bottom, then draped loosely to my ankles. The salesman had generously created a matching make-shift glove to cover the cast that I still donned on my wrist.

"Nice touch," James added, tapping the cast.

"You look quite spiffy yourself!" I giggled and jabbed him on the lapel of his dark grey Armani suit.

I looked over at my mother who was on the dance floor trying to teach Professor D how to dance salsa. "Look at them. They're hilarious!" I pointed at the duo and giggled. "Wanna dance?" Before I could take his hand, my phone rang. "Who the hell is this?" I thought aloud. The people closest to me, anyone who would have my new number, were all in the hall celebrating my graduation. I looked at the screen but didn't recognize the number. "Hello?"

"Hello stranger."

My blood turned to ice. I knew that voice anywhere. It was Fabian.

"How'd you get this number?" I asked frightened. I had changed my number and thought I'd ensured it was unlisted.

"I have my ways." He said coldly then his voice changed abruptly. "Look, I just called to say congratulations. You got what you always wanted, right?"

"That's right, no thanks to you." I felt suddenly brave. He was facing more than 50 years in prison. There was no way he could hurt me now.

Fabian snickered. "That's a gorgeous purple dress you're wearing."

My hands started to tremble so hard I almost dropped the phone. I whirled around, scanning the crowd, searching for who, I didn't know. "How? ... Who?" I stuttered.

"I'm glad to see you and your mom made up. Now you're a fuckin' happy family, huh?" he mocked frostily.

"*¡Hijo de tu máldita madre!*" I yelled. I heard Fabian laugh callously. Then all I heard was the dial tone.

36

I stared at the dilapidated building unable to decide on my next move. I was livid. I could feel my heart pounding in my throat, my nostrils flared. I held my tongue as I recalled the officer's words, "The call was traced to a Lynette Cintrón."

As soon as he saw the expression on my face, he knew the name was familiar to me. "Look, India, I wasn't supposed to give you this information. I could lose my job for this shit. Don't do anything stupid!"

I smiled, winked my eye and traced my finger behind his ear. His face flushed with embarrassment. I'd used my feminine wiles to get the detective to provide me with the confidential information.

I knew very well that Fabian couldn't have called me himself from the inside, that he'd have to have had someone three-way me. I also knew that the call could be traced rather easily. All it took was a flash of cleavage, fitted hip-hugger jeans and some good old-fashioned flirting, and I'd gotten the information I'd wanted. I didn't, however, expect Lynette's name to come out of the cop's mouth.

"Don't worry, pa. Your job isn't in any danger."

"Fabian won't be bothering you anymore, hun. He's been put in solitary, has ruined any remote chance he had of getting out on bail, and all his calls and mail are being monitored. You're safe now."

I laughed a hollow, ironic chuckle. "Safe? You don't know Fabian."

"We've been after that guy for years. You brought him down. We feel indebted to you, India. And you know I wouldn't let anything happen to that fine ass of yours." He licked his cracked lips. "So, when you gonna let me take you out for dinner, lady? You owe me, you know."

I faked a smile. This fat, balding Irish cop had no chance of ever bagging me. I did, however, find his confidence entertaining. "Let me take care of some things and I'll give you a call."

I planted a moist peck on his cheek and giggled as I walked out of the 34th precinct, his card in my hand. I took a cab straight to Lynette's building on Sherman Avenue.

As I sat in the car, I pondered what I should do. I knew I couldn't act recklessly. I had to plan this out. My revenge had to be sweet and neat. Several times, I almost bailed out, almost opted to just walk away from it all without taking any action but my pride didn't let me. My resentment fueled my will to get back at Lynette for her treachery. I had to at least confront her, tell her how I felt, how she'd hurt me.

My flight was booked. I'd reserved it the day after graduation. I had to get the fuck out of the city. I needed time away from everything and everybody; time to clear my head. But before I left, I had to take care of this last issue. I'd honestly been stunned by the revelation but as I thought about it further, not only did I become increasingly enraged, it also became clear that the news should not have come as such a huge shock. It's true that hindsight is 20/20. As I looked back, I realized that the chick had been jealous of me from jump. As my mother always said, *la envidia no mata pero sí mortifica,* envy is a torturous emotion.

I knew she'd fucked him while I was with him and now that I was putting the picture together, it was apparent they'd done more than fuck. They'd maintained a relationship all the while he and I were together. Now he was using her to get to me... I tried to calm myself down. I didn't want to resort to violence. I'd left that part of my life behind me when I left Bushwick to go to boarding school but at this point, I had little patience for anyone especially Lynette. The more I mulled over her betrayal, the more I felt she had to pay for being such a devious bitch. Her just deserts were long overdue.

Before going up to her apartment, I paid a Chinese delivery

guy to knock on her door. I had to make sure she was there and she was alone. When I received confirmation, I banged on her door.

"You order Chinese food," I asked with the best Chinese accent I could conjure.

She opened the door with an annoyed look on her mug. The minute she saw me, I saw fear in her eyes but she tried to conceal it with a grimace. "What the fuck do you want?"

I felt my boiling blood rush to my head. I took a deep breath in an effort to keep my hands to my side. I had instinctively coiled them into fists and was fighting the urge to pummel her.

"I came to talk to you. We have a lot discuss, don't you think?"

"Nice black eyes you got there." I glared at her as she taunted me, my nails cutting into my palms. "Did my boy Fabian do ..." I didn't let her finish her sentence. I punched her so hard in the mouth, the skin on my knuckles popped. I pushed my way into the apartment and pounced on her. I could no longer restrain myself.

I punched and kicked her until my body ached and sweat dripped from my brow. Then I collapsed against the wall and spat in her bloodied face as she whimpered.

"That's for fuckin' my man while you played like you was my girl and for helping him stalk me while he's locked up!" The thought rejuvenated me and I stood up and jumped on her again. She balled herself into fetal position and yelped with every kick.

Suddenly something came over me. It was like I was outside

myself; I saw my body flailing against Lynette's helpless form, the expression on my face was that of a mad woman who was taking extreme pleasure in the pain she was inflicting upon another. I backed up against the wall, tears cascaded from my eyes. I realized what I'd done, what I'd become. It wasn't that I felt bad for Lynette; she didn't deserve my empathy. It was more that in my frenzy to get back at her, I'd adopted some of Fabian's traits. I'd been sadistic and cruel and felt a strange euphoric joy knowing that I was causing Lynette physical anguish. The last person I wanted to be like was Fabian and there I was doing just that. I backed up towards the door and glared at Lynette's pitiful body.

"You were supposed to be my homegirl! I looked out for you! I was your only genuine friend! How could you?! Why did you have to do me like that? Why? What did I do to deserve that? I never fucked you over! I didn't do shit to deserve what you did! You knew how much I loved him, how I suffered for him! Why? Just tell me why!"

She stirred and looked at me through swollen eyes. She pushed her battered body up, spat some blood on the floor and wiped her face. With a sneer, she began her envy riddled rant.

"What about me, yo? Did you ever ask me how I felt? I'd loved that nigga for years before you came into the picture. I had a chance until you came along. Then you stole the spotlight. You were so fuckin' cute and skinny, had such potential. You had a future and a nigga that loved you. What the fuck did I have? I was a chubby high school dropout whose parents never gave a rat's ass about her! My mother beat the shit out of me while my father molested me! But you, you had it all and didn't see that. You didn't care about anything or anybody else. What did I have?" She collapsed and sobbed into her hands.

For the first time, I saw how truly pathetic Lynette was and I pitied her. I saw how life had defeated her and stolen her innocence. She didn't realize that she'd been disloyal to the only true friend she'd ever had, that she'd cheated herself. Instead of finding someone to love her, she'd focused all her energy on Fabian, on a love unrequited. She'd fallen into Fabian's trap in the same manner I had. She'd fallen victim to his charm and he preyed on her gullibility, on her passion for him. He'd used her time and time again and she permitted it and remained silent because in her eyes, he was all she had.

I looked around the studio apartment. The décor was drab, the furniture cheap. "You think that nigga really loved you? He didn't love either one of us, Lynette. He loved the control he had over us, that's what he loved. Damn girl, the least you could've done was get him to spend some money on you. This nigga got you livin' in a building that's falling apart, on furniture that looks secondhand. That's what you think you're worth? Being *'la otra'* while he had his *mujer* laced in a condo? I guess I never really knew you, huh?"

I shook my head simultaneously sympathetic and repulsed. "Now we're even. Stay the fuck away from me Lynette and stop helping that rat bastard. If you do, I'll know and I'll come for you."

I threw two hundred dollars on the floor next to her. "Go see a doctor and get yourself cleaned up. I'm sorry it had to go down like this." I walked out without a second look.

37

I sipped my Call a Cab mixed drink and looked out onto Ocean Drive from the second floor of Wet Willie's. When I'd decided to leave NYC, I knew immediately that I was heading to South Beach. The last time I'd felt free, I was in this city so I knew that's where I needed to be. The only person I'd told that I was leaving was my mom. I'd made her suffer enough. After everything I'd put her through, I didn't want to add insult to injury by having her worry about my whereabouts.

I inhaled deeply and allowed the crisp salty smell of the ocean to consume me. The past several months had been wrought with horror but I'd come out of it all sane and alive. I wasn't unscathed but I wasn't broken either. Although I didn't have a plan for my future, it didn't look as bleak as it had not too long ago and that knowledge appeased me. My ringing phone knocked me out of my revelry.

"What up, nena? What you doin'?"

Although I was happy to hear James's voice, I knew I didn't want to see him at the moment. "Nothing. I'm just chillin."

"What up yo? Let's get up for an L or something."

"Nah, I can't. I'm kinda… far."

"That's nothing. Just tell me where you at."

"James, I'm far, far, pa. Like out of the state far. I needed to get away." My voice trailed off. I didn't know what to say to James these days. We hadn't spoken about what happened between us but I knew it was on his mind. I loved him as my boy, for everything he'd done and continued to do for me, but I still wasn't sure if I could take it there with him and wasn't feeling up to considering it either.

"Oh it's like that. You just bounce and don't tell a nigga anything. India, it's me, J. I'm the one nigga in your life you can trust. Tell me you know that."

"It's not about you right now, pa. I don't know if you can understand that and I'm sorry. I just need to be alone right now. I need time for me."

"Yeah, aight. You take all the time you want." He hung up without waiting for further explanation. He was bitter but I had to focus on me, on healing, on reinvigorating myself.

I gulped the last of my drink and walked out onto Ocean Drive. I was deliberating taking a walk along the water when I felt a delicate touch on the small of my back. I turned and was shocked to see Anais beaming at me. She was certainly a sight for sore eyes.

"Muchacha, what are you doing down here?" she asked as she kissed me on the cheek.

"Living, girl, finally living."

I filled Anais in on the ghastly turn that my life had taken since our tryst. She listened stunned to tears as we walked along the water's edge but was elated to hear that I'd finally been able to claw Fabian out from under my skin. Before we knew it, the sun was rising over the horizon, heralding a new day.

"Damn, time flies when you're caught up in good conversation, huh?" I joked.

"So, where are you staying?"

"Oh, I have a suite at the Loews. I figure, I might as well spend Fabian's money spoiling myself."

"Shit *bella,* that nigga did so much foul shit to you, you still end up holding the short end of the stick if you ask me. No money is going to erase those scars he left on your soul."

"Well, I'm not trying to carry that baggage for the rest of my life. What happened, happened, you know. It's time for me to live, to be free. If I let those experiences dictate my every move, he'll have won. I have to move on."

"True that. So what are your plans?"

"I don't know. That's actually one of the reasons I came down here. To get my head straight and figure out what I'm going to do next. I have my whole life ahead of me. I can finally focus on me and that's what I intend on doing."

"No better day to start than today."

I smirked and kissed her on the forehead. "I'm glad I ran into you. I have an idea. How about we go freshen up and get some breakfast at the News Café. Then we can partake in one of my favorite pastimes - shopping."

"Sounds like a plan to me, *bella*."

We spent the next two weeks shopping at Miami's exclusive boutiques and enjoying the city's infamous nightlife.

38

To my relief, Anais didn't once try to push up on me. It's not that she wasn't attractive. Anais was one of the most gorgeous, sensual women I'd ever come across but considering what I'd been through, I just wasn't feeling up to being sexual with anyone. Although I'd planned on spending time alone, Anais was a welcome distraction. It felt good to have a female friend in my life. I hadn't had a genuine female counterpart since my friendship with Lynette. I'd forgotten how much fun it could be. We spent our days talking, tanning and shopping. Then we'd pretty ourselves up, and drink and dance the night away.

From our lengthy conversations I'd learned that like me,

Anais had come to Miami to escape her life in New York. When she'd first started stripping, she'd done it to put herself through school. Somewhere along the line, she'd gotten lost in the lure of money and drugs.

One day, during one of our late night talks she confided, "You know, you made me open my eyes, bella."

"How so?" I asked with a puzzled look.

"Well, that night we met, when you told me that you were about to graduate from college, I have to admit I was jealous. I mean, that's something I always wanted to do. Then I saw how your man abused you and that you did it in spite of your circumstances and I realized that I could do it too. But first I had to get out of the stripping world. That's why I'm here."

"So we're both running away from our demons. The only difference is that our demons have different faces but they're still demons." I took a deep tote from the L and passed it to her.

"I remember the first day I stripped like it was yesterday. I had to get piss drunk before I got on that stage. From day one I used alcohol to numb me, then I moved up to cocaine. The last night I was there, I saw this dancer OD. That's when I knew for sure I had to get out. I thought about you and what you were doing and it gave me hope."

"There's absolutely nothing you can't do if you set your mind to it girl. Nothing!" We stared at one another. For a quick second I felt the urge to kiss her but stopped myself. I knew I wasn't ready for intimacy. I jumped up and broke the awkward silence. "How about some seafood tonight? I'm starving!"

I spent the next few weeks fighting my impulses. I'd begun to question my sexuality. I'd never really considered it seriously until now. Was I a lesbian? There was no denying that I was enticed by beautiful women and Anais was striking. Her skin was the color of cinnamon, her features defined, and her eyes piercing. Her body was exquisite; her legs long and well-toned, her torso lean, breasts sumptuous. I would watch her as she dressed and noticed that she'd linger so that I could take her all in. After playing this game for several days, it was she who made the first move.

I stepped out of the shower to find her standing at the door. She scanned my bare body before saying in almost a whisper, "I've seen you watching me, India. I've been watching you too. I just..." I kissed her before she could finish.

At first the kisses were slow and deliberate. They soon became increasingly intense and passionate. Our hands roamed flesh while we blindly made our way to the bed.

"It's my turn!" I exclaimed with a seductive wink. I lay her down on the bed and went to work. I ran my hands through her hair while I kissed her neck. I moved on to her breasts, using my hands to hold them together while I alternated licking each nipple with the tip of my tongue. I watched her bite her lip with ecstasy. Little by little, I made my way down her torso, lightly sucking every inch of her warm skin. Her Brazilian wax made my mouth water in anticipation.

I put my finger to her lips and whispered, "Guide me." She smiled and obeyed. I followed her, doing to her clitoris what she did to my finger. I grazed my lips and tongue over her clit and felt her shiver. I took her into my mouth and began to stimulate her with circular motions, entwining my tongue with her clit, first slowly then with increasing vigor. I began to flick her clit in a vertical motion, making it a point to lick its full length before moving down. As I took it into my mouth and began to suck and gyrate, I placed a finger into her and found her G-spot. She moaned and her body stiffened. I continued to tease her, first moving my mouth and finger slow then fast then slow again when I felt her nearing climax. I finally relented when she yelped in desperation. I took her into my mouth and flitted my tongue rapidly over her clitoris while I stroked her G-spot with mounting intensity. Anais grabbed my hair and screamed while she came, her juices squirted and dripped down my chin and hand.

"India. Oh my God, India!" she yelled in delight as I continued eating until goose bumps rose on her flesh. She dissolved into a panting heap when I resurfaced. I wiped the sweat from her forehead and smiled at her.

"We're not done yet, Missy."

She whimpered when she saw me take out my trusty buddy, a vibrator equipped with a prong for clitoral stimulation. Before she could contest, I had taken her pussy into my mouth again.

I waited until Anais's eyes were closed in rapture before introducing my toy. As soon as she heard it, her eyes shot open. "I've never tried one of those," she admitted with a pout.

"Oh, you'll love it, precious. Just relax." She acquiesced, loosening her muscles and closing her eyes. I introduced the vibrator delicately, alternating between the toy and my tongue. When I felt her respond, I increased the use of the vibrator, watching her contort as I thrusted in slow motions. She shrieked loudly begging me to stop but I knew that it was the opposite she really wanted. I watched her as she peaked again, a sweet smile on her lips, eyes clenched shut.

"I've never in my life had such an intense orgasm," she whispered in between gasps and giggles.

I took her into my arms and cradled her. Before I knew it, she was asleep. I looked into her magnificent face and wondered if I could ever fall in love with a woman, with this woman. As I stared at her, a pang of guilt struck me. I was suddenly aware that I hadn't considered Anais's feelings. I wasn't trying to hurt anyone in my quest to find myself. I placed her gently onto the pillow and walked out onto the balcony.

The night was warm and star strewn. I could hear the ocean crashing against the shore and could just make out figures walking along the beach. I leaned against the railing and stared out into the night.

What am I doing? What is it I want? I just slept with this

woman with no thought as to how she's feeling. Could I be with her or any woman for that matter? On a deeper level than just a sexual one? I stretched and felt the weeks of insufficient rest overcome me. I lay down next to Anais and watched her steady breathing form until my eyes closed in slumber.

I awoke the next morning relieved to find that I was alone in bed. I found Anais sitting on the balcony sipping coffee. She'd ordered every breakfast item on the menu unsure of what I'd prefer. She'd also found the time to get a lavish bouquet of wild orchids. She'd picked some out and laid them ornately around the table. The entire scene looked grandiose against the splendid blue of the cloudless sky. It was also far too romantic for my confused state. I reluctantly sidled to my seat and sat down with a slight frown on my face. I tried to appear grateful but my lack of enthusiasm was difficult to hide.

"Look India, I only did this to thank you for giving me the most incredible orgasms of my life." Anais giggled trying to lighten the tense mood.

I smiled and looked at her. Even with her hair disheveled and no makeup, Anais was naturally dazzling. Guilt ate away at me.

"Anais, I ..."

"Don't India. I know what happened yesterday was just a moment. You don't have to explain it to me. You're going through some craziness right now. You don't have to add me to the clutter in your head. I'm here for you as a friend, *bella*."

"It wasn't just a moment, Anais. I'm just not sure where my heart is right now. I honestly don't know if I can ever be with a woman beyond the sex, you know."

"I know exactly what you mean. I went through that myself. I came to realize that I'm bisexual. That's just me though."

"I don't know if it's that simple though. There's just so many gray areas. I mean, I don't see myself settling down with a woman but that doesn't mean that I'm not attracted to women. Does that mean I'm bisexual or have bisexual tendencies?" I groaned at my annoying habit of over-thinking.

"In essence darling, you're straight. It is that simple, bella."

I sighed and looked out onto the ocean. The clear blue waters enticed me.

"How about we go for a swim? I need some salt on my body."

"I'm down. If you ask me India, and I know you haven't, but *bella* you're not gay. It's just not in you."

I looked at her perplexed; how did she know what I'd been thinking? I was too tired of breaking my head to try to figure it out. I grabbed a bagel, kissed her on the forehead and walked into the suite to dress for the beach.

I watched the glistening bodies walk by me as I lay out tanning. It was like 90% of the population of Miami Beach were either gym fiends or had spent thousands of dollars in plastic surgery making their bodies perfect. The men had chiseled physiques with eight pack abdominals. The women had perky, abundant breasts and their tight glutes were accentuated by the thongs they donned. It was a feast for the eyes. While I ogled, I thought about my dilemma.

I imagined what life might be like with a woman. Intimacy with a female was completely different; a woman's touch was more tender, an encounter more delicate and stimulating on a more aesthetic level. On the other hand, sex with a man was a carnal pleasure I found irresistible. There was something about the rougher hand of a man, the feeling of being protected and dominated. The more I thought about it, the more I envisaged my life with a man. I turned to Anais who'd been watching me for I didn't know how long.

"You know, you were grinding your teeth in your sleep last night. I'm surprised you didn't gnash them to the root."

"Yeah, I do that when I'm stressed," I responded.

"So, have you come to any decisions?" she inquired with curiosity.

"Um..."

"Let me guess, you see your life with a man, right?"

Again I was mystified by her ability to read my mind. "What do you have ESP or something?"

"Yeah, I'm a witch *bella,* didn't you know?" she laughed. "Nah, we've just talked so much over these past few weeks that I feel like I know you. Girl, you're the 'get married and have kids' type. And there's nothing wrong with that."

"I think you're right. There's just nothing like a man."

"You know, I have to agree but there's also nothing like a woman."

"Very true." I sipped my drink and turned my gaze to the eye candy that crossed my view.

39

When we got back to the room, I soaked in a tub of eucalyptus and aloe essence. It struck me that I hadn't thought about Fabian in days. This was perhaps the first time in years that I'd spent so extended a period without him in the forefront of my mind. I was proud of myself but at the same time, my heart palpitated at the mental image of him. I quickly jumped out of the bath and entered the room.

I was almost bowled over by the scene that was waiting for me. Anais had lit candles all around the room and scattered rose petals on the bed. She reclined seductively on the burgundy suede divan opposite the bed clad in a bone colored negligee, thigh highs and stiletto sandals. In one hand, she sipped what looked like champagne with cherries. With the other hand, she clutched the remote. Unexpectedly, Amber's "Sexual" began to play in the background. Anais walked over to me and led me to the divan.

"Remember this song?"

"How could I forget?" She'd danced this song for me on the day we met at Sue's. I smiled at the memory.

"This is what I imagined as I danced for you that night." She began to sway her body in front of me. "I want to show you how I wanted it to be between just you and me. Can I show you?" She whispered this into my ear as she brushed her body against mine.

I didn't answer. I couldn't. I was spellbound. She stepped away and began to move, her hands glided over her body. In her years of stripping, Anais had gotten this down to an art form. She turned around and bounced her ass cheeks as she loosened her hair from its high ponytail, letting it fall down her back. She then turned around swiftly and fell to her knees. She crawled to me, mouthing the words to the song as she made her way. "You say how much you value our friendship/ but aren't you addicted to my perfume."

She inched her way in between my legs and traced the contours of my face with her fingertip. She grazed her lips against mine as she opened my robe and let it hang loosely off my shoulders, exposing my taut nipples. She took one into her mouth as she massaged the other in between two fingers. My breathing became labored as I tried to control myself.

She stroked my torso with wet kisses as she moved linearly

towards my craving, hairless pussy. She wasted no more time. She began to eat me with force, taking my entire clitoris into her mouth, massaging it with the length of her tongue. I threw my head back and groaned with delight. I felt tingles all over my body. I clenched the divan with my fists and curled my toes as I felt myself ready to explode. To my thrilled surprise, she didn't let me peak just yet. She retreated and entered me with her index finger and began to thrust into me. I gasped for air, biting my lower lip in desperation and moaning loudly. She then took me entirely into her mouth again, stimulating my clitoris with both her tongue and her lips, her head shaking as she tortured me. I screamed as I felt myself explode. She wrapped her arms around my thighs so that I couldn't pull away, making me orgasm several more times in succession. Tears streamed from my eyes as my hairs stood on end and my body buckled exhausted onto the divan.

When I opened my eyes again, it was early morning. I'd unintentionally fallen asleep after the countless orgasms. I turned to see Anais nestled next to me. My mistress of seduction had apparently tired herself out as well.

I pulled away slowly so as not to wake her and walked out onto the balcony. I could hear the feint sounds of parties going on below. I was no longer beguiled by the sounds. I'd done enough partying in the past few weeks to last me a lifetime.

At once I understood that it was time for me to leave. Time for me to go back to New York, to face what I'd been running from. I rolled a small blunt and puffed it while I watched the sunrise. The splendor of the swirl of colors against the expanse of ocean reassured me. I was finally certain that I was ready to tackle my demons. I was tired of running. My time away had served it's purpose. I was once again whole, something I hadn't been in a long time. Although the impending still frightened me to some extent, I was no longer afraid to confront it. I'd gathered my strength. I'd revived my spirit and wanted to seize the moment.

I heard Anais's footsteps behind me and passed her the L without looking. She took it and sat next to me, put her head on my shoulder and sighed.

"You're ready, aren't you?"

"Yet again you baffle me with your ability to peer into my mind." We faced one another. "I don't know if I could have done it without you, *preciosa.*" I tenderly pushed her hair behind her ears. "You are a true friend and I hope that we will always remain."

"You were always ready, *bella.* You're stronger than you realize. I knew last night when I seduced you." She giggled. "It was our last hurrah as they say." She gestured the air with the L as if toasting. "I'll be a phone call away if anything but this is where I need to be right now."

"I know. I'll miss you though." I kissed her on the forehead and hugged her tightly, blinking back the tears.

"Don't start that shit, girl." She shoved me away and pursed her lips. "This is an 'I'll see you later' not a goodbye, understand?"

"No doubt." We looked out onto the horizon and smoked in silence as the sun bared it's full form.

40

I was so immersed in writing in my new journal that I almost missed my flight. Anais had bought me a lovely new writing book as a going away gift. "Write it all down," she said as she kissed me goodbye. I could swear I saw her wipe her eyes as she walked away but I couldn't be sure.

My heart began to race when I boarded the plane but I found solace in my journal. The effects were instantly therapeutic. I wrote without thinking. I simply let my pen glide across the paper. It did so with ease, drawing inspiration from the bizarre and often time ghastly events that I'd endured in the past several years of my life. Before I knew it, the pilot announced that we were landing in several minutes.

The sight of the infamous New York skyline brought a smile to my face. I became conscious of how much I'd missed my home, my city. It felt good to be back. There was much to do and I was going to waste no time doing it. I knew what my first destination would be.

Professor Daines opened the door in her nightgown. She rubbed her eyes and looked at me through squinting eyes. It was well past midnight. I knew she'd probably be sleeping but I was too anxious to see her so I showed up at her apartment.

"Child, what in the world are you doing knocking on my door at this obscene hour?" she said half-joking. She embraced me firmly and led me into her kitchen. "Let me make us some coffee. I have a feeling what you're about to tell me is intense and I want to be fully alert for it."

"No need for coffee, Professor Daines... I mean Joanna," I corrected myself quickly in response to her stern look. "Nothing ghastly has occurred, not since, well, you know ..."

Joanna put her hand on my shoulder and gave it a comforting squeeze. "I'm not used to being up at this hour, honey. I don't mind if it's for you but this woman is getting old. I need coffee to keep my eyes open and my head steady." She chuckled. "You talk while I put a pot on."

"Do you think I'm too young to write a memoir?"

Joanna stopped scooping the grinds into the coffee maker and turned to look at me with an enormous grin. "You're never too young to write a memoir. At least I don't think so. And from what I know about your life, you certainly have enough material."

"Well, I've been thinking about what you've told me for years. You know, that I should consider a career in writing and I thought why the hell not. I've been writing my entire life. I mean, I haven't really written in some time because my mind's been preoccupied with other things. I don't need to explain that cuz you know all too well. Anyway, today I picked up a pen and I haven't been able to stop. It was like a dam had been holding back this tremendous flow, and now the dam is splintered and I can't hold back the surge. I really think I've got something here."

"You have so much more than you realize. Wait here for a minute. I just have to go to my study." She returned with several thick, overstuffed folders and passed them to me. I stared at her confused. "Well, open them silly."

I was astounded to find that it was all the writing I'd ever submitted to her over the years. Everything from flows of consciousness we'd done in class to papers she'd assigned. I flipped through the pages, some slightly yellowed with age. My mouth was open with wonder and amazement.

"You saved all of this?" I said at last. "Why? I mean, I don't understand."

"Because I saw a young woman who had an immense untapped talent. I saw a woman who I knew would one day come into herself as a true writer. And I was right, wasn't I? Here you are. You've realized that you have an amazing gift that even I envy. India, you have an ability to weave a tale that I am convinced some of the most well-known writers of yesterday and today would encourage you hone. This is your calling. Run with it. I'll help you in every way I possibly can."

I choked on the knot in my throat. I hugged her so tight, she actually pleaded that I release her. We talked over coffee into the wee hours of the morning.

41

I spent the next few weeks roaming the vibrant streets of New York. I walked, rollerbladed and rode my bike all around the city, stopping wherever I found inspiration – in cafés, parks, malls, the subway, wherever my muse nudged me for attention, I stopped and let my pen fly. I still hadn't called James and felt totally guilty about it but I didn't yet feel ready to face him. I missed him to pieces but seeing him meant I had to break his heart more than I already had and I couldn't bring myself to do that just yet.

One evening, after a full day of bike riding, Purple Lights, my spot in Battery Park, beckoned me. As I approached, I at once felt a heartwarming nostalgia and a pang of distress. The last time I'd been here, I'd been kidnapped and raped shortly thereafter. Still, the spot held so many uplifting memories for me. It had been the place I'd fled to when I needed to get away from Fabian. The energy of the place had also always stirred my creative juices.

I sat on a bench and took out my journal. I noticed that there was a fellow bike rider sitting on a bench not too far from me but I thought nothing of it. My muse was prodding me so I folded my legs beneath me and gave in. Minutes later, a familiar voice got my attention.

"Something told me that I'd see you again one day but I never thought it would be here." I looked up and couldn't believe my eyes. "India, right? I could never forget that name and most definitely not that stunning face."

"Ruben?" I stared at him open mouthed. This was the guy I'd met on the train what seemed like years ago. I'd met him the day I met Anais, shortly before my world came tumbling down around me. He'd struck me then as the type of guy I needed and wanted in my life - educated, polite, extremely handsome, and eloquent.

"Wow, you remember my name. That is the ultimate compliment." He leaned his bike against the railing next to mine and sat next to me.

"You were sitting over there the whole time?" I pointed to the spot where I'd seen a figure earlier.

"I'd been sitting there for a while, yes. I was reading and just enjoying the view. I love this place. Been coming here for years. I discovered it when I was student at NYU."

"Really? I've been coming here for years as well. It's the energy of the place that lures me."

"Interesting, don't you think? That we've both been coming here for so long and have never run into one another."

"I believe everything happens for a purpose."

"I must agree," he said with a nod. "So, how've you been?"

"Better." He looked at me quizzically. I was alluding to the fact that I was no longer with Fabian but didn't want to come out and just say it. I remembered that at our last encounter, he'd flirted with me only to find out that I was involved. We'd both been disappointed.

"So, you're a bike rider, I see. Yet another thing we have in common." He looked towards the setting sun and back at me. "So India, tell me, how have you really been?"

"I'm okay now but I wasn't okay for a while but that doesn't matter anymore. That's in the past."

He nodded pensively still looking at me with his piercing eyes. "You're single now then?"

"What gave it away?" I asked with a shy smile.

"There's just something different about you. You're lighter, like you're not carrying any burdens anymore, that's it. Your aura is different. You seem lighter."

"Truer words have never been spoken. I am definitely lighter."

"So, now that you've shed yourself of those chains that once bound you, would you like to join me for a cappuccino or maybe a smoothie? Your choice."

I'd forgotten what it felt like to meet someone new. Butterflies fluttered in my stomach and my palms became sweaty. My heart tickled my breast as I tried to respond without collapsing into schoolgirl giggles. "I'd love a smoothie and I know just the place."

We talked for hours as we walked through SoHo and Greenwich Village. Before we knew it, it was dawn. Although I tried not to reveal too much about my life, I ended up telling him more than I'd expected. He was so easy to talk to and so engaging. I was scared as I told him of my relationship with Fabian. After all, he was an educated man and I feared that he would judge me, that he'd question my own intelligence. I was wrong. He revealed that he grew up on the streets and had changed his life when he witnessed his brother fall victim to the streets.

"You're one of the smart ones for being able to get out of it when you did. Pat yourself on the back for that, India." He wiped the solitary tear that rolled down my cheek.

When I told him of the kidnapping, his nostrils flared with anger. "That nigga's not a man. A real man doesn't put his hands on a woman. That shows how weak he truly is. I hope he rots in jail for what he did to you. He deserves worse but the world has a way of getting you back for your sins. I'm a strong believer in karma. Let the cosmos take care of him."

"I can't believe I told you all that I have," I confessed.

"You have nothing to be ashamed of, India. We all make mistakes in life. My mom always told me that it doesn't matter that you fall off the ladder, what matters is that you get up and climb it again."

I learned that he was a graphic designer and photographer and had started his own business several years back. The more I talked to him, the more I liked him and the more I wanted to get to know him. Unknowingly, he had begun to knock down the walls I'd built around my heart for fear of further suffering.

I gasped when I realized the hour. "Broke your curfew?" he joked.

"No, it's not that. I just can't believe we've been talking for so long. I feel like…" I stopped myself before finishing. I didn't want to scare him away.

"Like you've known me for a long time," he finished my sentence for me. "I feel the same way, India. You don't have to hold yourself back. I'm not going anywhere. So, where you at right now? I mean, where are you staying?"

"Well, I've been staying with my mentor. She's been helping me with my writing. I think I told you about her." He nodded. "But I'm looking for a place in the area around Columbia University."

"I'm uptown on 145th for now but I'm about to buy a condo in Riverdale. Wanna ride the train together?"

We talked during the ride uptown and when I said goodbye, I was tempted to kiss him but felt that I had to take it slow. Ruben didn't try to push up on me. He pecked me on the forehead and promised to call me in a couple of hours.

I jumped for joy as I walked through the streets. It didn't matter that it was pouring rain. Nothing could rain on my parade at that moment.

42

I was in a love stricken haze for the next few weeks. I spent my days writing and apartment hunting and my evenings with Ruben. He courted me respectfully, opening doors for me, pulling my chair out so I could sit down, walking me home after our dates and kissing me on the forehead when he departed.

One evening he called and invited me to a spoken word event at the Nuyorican Poets Café. I had to go see an apartment on 85th Street so I asked him to join me and we could leave from there.

As soon as I saw the brownstone, I knew that I'd love the apartment. I walked in and fell in love with the exposed brick of the walls. The high ceilings gave the one bedroom a spacious, art studio feel. I turned to look at Ruben with arched eyebrows.

"This is it," he read my mind.

"I'll take it!" I shrieked before the realtor could say any more.

I was so excited I threw my arms around Ruben and planted a firm kiss on his lips. I jumped back when I realized what I'd done. "I'm sorry."

"Don't apologize. It was nice." He smiled at me and drew me close to him. He nestled his nose in my neck and inhaled deeply. "You smell nice."

I blushed and held him to me. "Shall we go?" He put my hand in his as we walked down the block.

"That apartment has India written all over it."

"I know. I knew it as soon as I saw the building."

The Nuyorican was jumping with excitement when we walked in. I was surprised to see that everyone appeared to know Ruben. He introduced me as his special friend, and squeezed my hand and winked at me affectionately when I looked at him embarrassed. We sat in front and took in the performances with zeal. I would never have predicted what happened next.

"Our next performer is one of my old time favorites. He's been frequenting this spot for years now, blessing us with his lyrics.

Let's give a hearty round of applause for my boy, Ruben Sanchez."

The crowd erupted with whoops and hollers and loud applause. I turned to look at Ruben who gave me a sly grin as he got up and walked up to the podium.

"What's up, y'all? How ya been? Sorry I haven't been here in a minute but a nigga been busy. This one is gonna be a little different from my usual spits. See, I have a new being in my life. She is my muse, my personal Erato." He looked at me with softness and winked.

I met her some time ago and was struck by her – not by her beauty though she was fine. What hit me hard was the invisible weight she carried on her back. The weight of the world it seemed. So gorgeous yet so sad. I immediately wanted to protect her, save her from the dark cloud that loomed over her head. But that wasn't my place, it wasn't my time. So I let that lady walk away and hoped that one day, our paths would meet again. And my prayers were answered y'all 'cause the other day, she came to me, I came to her. We met again but the woman I saw was different. She was no longer the woman I'd met that day some time ago. She was stronger. Bruised but more alive as a result of it. That woman didn't need me to save her, she saved herself. She freed herself. And then she came into my world to free me. See, I had my own weight I was carrying, my own dark cloud over my head. She came and tossed that weight asunder, chased the cloud away with her light. Her light that would blind all evil and despair. She doesn't know that she met a man that was scared, unwilling to open up, to feel, to want. In an instant, she made me want to, need to open up to her, to show her what I have, all that I am. This man that's standing in front of you today, is a different man, more of man because of her, Indiecita mía. And now I want to do for her what she's done for me, protect her, respect her, be there and stay there. All for my little India.

I was frozen in my seat. The passion with which he performed his ode gave me chills. The audience craned their necks trying to see who Ruben was looking at as he recited. When he was done, they clapped and whistled their enjoyment. I stared at Ruben as he walked towards me, grinning from ear to ear. My hands were shaking and my stomach churned; I had never in my life had such poetic words dedicated to me. He put his hand out to me. I took it and rose from my seat, still dumbfounded. Right there, in front of at least a hundred people, we shared our first kiss. It was the most intense yet most delicate kiss I'd ever had in my life and I couldn't believe the circumstances under which it was happening. The crowd hooted and hollered, screaming in unison, "*Que se besen! Que se besen!*"

"Why didn't you tell me you were a poet?" I whispered.

"Would you have had it any other way?"

I realized I wouldn't have had it any other way at all.

43

The following week Ruben helped me move in to my new place and shop for furniture. Though we spent hours making out, we still hadn't slept together and he made no attempt to do so. The manner in which he respected me made me want him more but I knew that taking it slow was the best thing for us.

One night, after I was all moved in, I finally spoke to him about James. I didn't mention that we'd slept together. That was an unnecessary detail that I didn't think he needed to know. I did admit that James had confessed his love for me. He listened quietly when I explained all he'd done for me and how guilty I felt for being unable to reciprocate the emotion.

"I love him dearly. He's my best friend and he's done so much for me, put his own neck on the line but I'm not in love with him and know I could never love him like that."

"Have you told him that, India? He deserves to know so he can move on."

"No, I haven't told him. I just feel so bad."

"For what? You can't control who you love. You don't pick love, love picks you. You should call him. Go see him and talk to him."

I looked at this man who seemed to understand me the way no man ever had, not even James. I felt so lucky, like I'd finally been rewarded for all that I'd suffered.

"You're beautiful, you know that, right? Inside and out." I pecked him on the lips.

"So are you, *Indiecita*. It's about time you realize that and stop being so hard on yourself. Call him. I'm gonna go. I have a long day tomorrow. I'll call you when I get home."

I didn't want him to go. I wanted him to stay with me. I wanted to feel him so bad, it was torture but I knew we couldn't, shouldn't. I walked him to the door and kissed him deeply.

"Mmmmmmm. Girl..." He shook his head and I knew he was thinking was I was thinking. "Let me go, India. I'll see you tomorrow."

I watched him from my window as he walked up the block

and thought about the advice he'd given me. I exhaled deeply and grabbed the phone. It was now or never.

As soon as I heard his voice on the line, tears leaked from my eyes, bathing the front of my shirt.

"James," I said softly. "I'm so sorry, James. Please forgive me." There was a moment of silence on the line.

"Its okay, India. It hurts but I understand." Those words caused a second flood of tears but these were of relief.

We met the next day for lunch. I ran to him when I saw him crossing the street. He looked great. He'd put on some weight but he looked healthy and happy.

"So how've you been? What have you been up to? How's life? Details, details!"

He laughed at me. "You're the same spastic chick you always were."

"I haven't changed that much, James."

"Well, I finished that internship at Sony and they opted to hire me."

"That's what's up!"

"Yeah, that's exciting. I'll be making great money and doing what I enjoy – programming. They're also paying for my masters so I'll probably be going back to school in a couple of months."

"Cool. Cool. So is that's what has you looking so good?" I squeezed his bicep teasingly.

"Yeah that and..." he hesitated.

"What? What is it? You can tell me. It's me."

"I met somebody."

"Wow! That's dope! So tell me all about her."

"I don't know if I feel comfortable doing that."

"Why? Don't be silly. You would've told me before, why not now?"

"A lot has changed, India. I told you I loved you *nena*, or did you forget?"

"No, I didn't forget. I guess I'd hoped it wouldn't have changed our friendship but I guess I was wrong."

He sighed. "Well, her name is Cynthia. She works at Sony as a programmer as well. I met her in the internship program. She's Puerto Rican, just graduated from Cornell, great girl. She's got her shit together, you know."

"No doubt. She sounds like a great girl. Good luck with that."

"There's more."

I waited silently not knowing what to expect but it didn't sound good.

"Well, um, her family lives in L.A. and she asked for a transfer to the branch over there. They gave it to her. Are even going to give her moving expenses, gonna set her up with a crib and everything.

She asked me to go with her. I said yes."

"Wow. That's huge. Are you ready for that, James?" I didn't know how to feel. I wondered if he was leaving to get away from me.

"I need to start fresh. And she's a good girl. We're not going to move in together or anything. I'll have my place, she'll have hers but if she goes across the country and I stay here, there's just no way it'll work. I just feel like I have to give this a try."

"I understand. Well, follow your heart. If that's the right thing for you right now, go for it."

"Yeah, follow my heart." He rolled his eyes. I didn't dare question him further. We continued our lunch in silence. I picked at my Caesar's salad. Somehow, I'd lost my appetite.

"So, are you planning on telling me about this new guy you're dating?"

I almost choked on a crouton. "How did you ..."

"C'mon, India. I've known you for how many years now. You're fuckin' glowing. I almost mistook you for a fuckin' beacon, you're so radiant." His sarcasm burned right through me.

"Um, well yeah, I did meet someone."

"You didn't just meet someone. You've fallen in love. It's written all over your pretty little face." His tone was arctic.

I couldn't stand his cutting bitterness. I felt bad for not sharing his feelings but he was being unreasonable. Still I tried to understand him and not be offended, after all he was the one nursing wounds I'd inflicted.

"I am involved with someone. I don't know where it's going but I am hopeful. He's a good man and he's wonderful to me. I'm sorry."

"What are you apologizing for?" he interrupted apprehensively. "So you met someone. That's great. So have you learned how to treat a good man or are you going to chase this one away as well?"

I couldn't take his spitefulness anymore. I slammed my fork on the table and glared at him. "You know what, James? I'm sorry that I hurt you and that I couldn't reciprocate how you felt but you don't have to be so fucking nasty to me. I don't deserve that. You know everything I've been through and you have the audacity to play victim. How dare you? It's me, India. Your best friend for years. What the fuck is your problem?" I blinked back the tears that gathered at the corners of my eyes. I refused to give him the pleasure of seeing me cry.

"India, I haven't heard from you since when? We're not friends anymore, who are you kidding? You decided you needed to do you so while you were doing that, I did me. I'm sorry if you don't like the way I'm talking to you or treating you. This is me now. Don't be so fucking sensitive."

"Sensitive?" I couldn't believe my ears. I gaped at James but he refused to meet my eyes. He was resentful and there wasn't much I could do about it. This was something he was going to have to cope with and get over on his own.

"I think it's time for me to go. It was, um, nice to see you again. You take care." I could no longer sit there and take his abuse. My departure was cold to say the least. I could feel him watching me as I walked out of the restaurant but his pride didn't let him apologize or run after me. I didn't wait for him to do so either. I called Ruben as soon as I exited the restaurant.

"Don't worry about it, India *mía*. There's nothing you can do for him. He's a man and has to do what's right for him. You did your part."

"Yeah, I know. I just feel… I don't know."

"Forget about that. How about I make you dinner tonight?"

"Damn, pa, you cook too? I am too lucky to have you."

"I think we're both lucky, India. I'll pick up some stuff at Citarella before I head over there later. You gonna be okay?"

"Yes. I'll be fine now that I have you."

"And you certainly do have me, India. Besos. I'll talk to you in a little while."

As had become the custom, Ruben assuaged my every worry and smoothed away my frown lines.

44

I spent my entire afternoon on my new writing chair enveloped in the world of my journal. By then I had filled six journals with the stories of my life. Without realizing it, I fell asleep curled in a ball, pen perched precariously in my hand, book on my lap. I awoke to a tap on the door.

"India? You there? Open up."

My cheeks tickled at the sound of his voice. I jumped up and opened the door. The sight of him, loaded with bags, soaked from the apparent downpour, made me giggle. "Oh baby, you look like a wet dog." I planted a quick kiss on his lips before running for a towel but before I could wrap him in it, he swept me off my feet. Cradling me, he kissed me softly.

"How's my Indiecita doing? You feeling better?"

As I looked at him, I felt like little ladybugs were dancing around in my chest making my skin prickle. "I'm wonderful now that you're here."

He smirked and put me down, grabbed the bags and headed towards the kitchen. I followed him, towel in hand.

"How does seafood sound? We'll start off with a shrimp cocktail, butter and garlic dipped lobster tail with wild rice. For dessert, strawberry cheesecake."

"Pa, you're gonna get me fat." I laughed as I tousled his hair with the towel.

"We'll worry about that later. There's a gym on Amsterdam I was looking at. I thought we could join it together. How does that sound?" He put the bags down on the countertop and turned to me. He wrapped his arms around my waist and nuzzled his nose in my neck, his trademark demonstration of affection. "Oooh, somebody needs a shower."

"Shut up." I smacked him softly on the chest. "I didn't get a chance." I whined. "I came home and started writing. I think I'm getting close to being done."

"Really? That's dope. Well, get some stuff together for me so I can read it after dinner. In the meantime, go wash that pretty little ass. You smell like sweat." He smacked me softly on the bottom.

"Wait. I have something for you." I ran to my desk and

retrieved a small box from the drawer. I'd bought it several days before but hadn't found the opportune moment to give it to him.

"What's this?" he asked crinkling his brow with curiosity.

"Open it and see."

He opened it and retrieved two keys. "What's this? The keys to your heart?" He held his hands dramatically to his chest. "Kinda corny don't you think?"

"No, that would have been kind of high school of me. Um, there's a key to the lobby door and the other is a key to my door." I scrutinized his face for a reaction. I'd worried that the step was premature. I mean we hadn't even slept together yet but my instincts told me it was right so I followed my gut.

He looked at the keys and looked at me intently, then back at the keys. "Wow, India. I don't know what to say."

"Well, you're always here anyway. I just thought ..." I was growing increasingly anxious, concerned that he'd think I was rushing him. The last thing I wanted was to scare him away. He kissed me before I could start panicking.

"Indiecita, are you ready for this?"

"What do you mean am I ready? I was worried that you wouldn't be ready."

"Me, not ready? Girl, I'm waiting for you. You don't have to wait for me. The ball's in your court."

I tilted my head to the side, taking in his confession. "I'm ready honey."

He nodded and kissed my forehead. Just then the bell rang. "Who could that be?" he asked with a sneaky snigger.

"I'm not expecting anyone." I walked to the door and spoke into the intercom.

"Delivery from CompUSA."

"Huh?" I buzzed the guy in. "You expecting a delivery, babe?"

"Are you?" I recognized the playful twinkle in his eye. The knock on the door stopped me from inquiring further.

When I opened the door my eyes made their way to the two boxes at the deliveryman's feet. "Delivery for an India Maldonado."

"I didn't order anything."

"Just sign for it, India."

I gave Ruben a 'what are you up to' face as I signed for the package. Ruben handed the guy a tip and brought the packages into the living room. I followed him, crazy with curiosity.

"So, are you going to open it or stand there and gawk at me?"

"What did you do?"

"Just open it!" he commanded exasperated, a little laugh in the back of his throat.

I began to pull away the packing paper and fell on my ass when I saw what it was. There on the box was a picture of an HP laptop.

"Now open the other one, please."

The other box contained an HP printer. I sat speechless looking at the boxes. My gift couldn't, didn't compare to his.

"I know this doesn't compare to the key but I just thought you could start fresh with a new computer and printer. You're starting a new *época* in your life India, writing your first book and everything. I thought some new equipment would help you along. You can take the laptop with you everywhere you go." He kneeled and started opening the box. "It's really lightweight. I ordered a bag for it. They're on backorder but should arrive within two days or so the salesman said."

I threw my arms around him, knocking him over. "It's perfect!" I showered his face with kisses. I straddled him and pinned his arms over his head. "And what do you mean this doesn't compare to the key? This is too much. You really shouldn't have."

He flipped me over quickly. "India, you gave me a key to your crib. Yeah, my gift was more expensive but yours was... Trust me, there's no comparison."

Feeling him on top of me felt amazing. His manhood rubbed against my belly and I felt flutters in my private. I blushed and tried to wrestle him off. He tickled me until I pleaded for mercy then kissed me, pulling me up close to him. I could feel his longing as he rubbed his arms up and down my side. Suddenly he pulled away, lifting us both to our feet.

"I've got to make dinner. You go take a shower, stinky." I watched him as he walked to the kitchen. I knew he felt what I felt, he wanted to feel me as much as I wanted to feel him but he was holding himself back, waiting for me.

I walked to the bathroom with a pout. Were we ready? Was our relationship ready? There I go over-thinking again, I scolded.

Dinner was extraordinary. Ruben made me stay in the living room while he prepared the dining area. He'd lit dozens of candles all around and had arranged a bouquet of colorful African violets as a centerpiece. The food looked and tasted mouth-watering.

We fed one another in between bites. When he brought out the cheesecake, I looked at him with suspicion. "That looks incredibly like a Junior's cheesecake."

He laughed with guilt. "Okay, okay. This I didn't make. It is from Junior's but everything else was my doing."

"Strawberry cheesecake is my favorite." I cut a small piece and put it to his mouth. He licked it from my fingers, eyes fixed on mine. He cupped my face and sucked my lips. Gooseflesh spread on my arms. Then he stopped himself.

"Why are you so scared to touch me, babe?"

"Scared? India, with everything you've told me, I don't want to rush you into anything. I'm dying to, you have no idea, but I want it to be right for both of us, not just for me."

We ate our dessert in silence. Afterward, he went to work

arranging my new computer and printer on my desk. He pulled off his button down and worked in his wife-beater. The muscles on his arms and shoulders flexed as he labored. I had to squeeze my hands in between my thighs to keep from touching him.

"I'm gonna go take a shower, India," he said when he was done constructing my new workstation. He hugged me and snuggled into my neck. "Mmmm, now you smell scrumptious and I stink. Let me take a quick shower and we'll watch a movie."

I watched his broad shoulders enter my bathroom. I had no intention of watching a movie that night.

I took off my clothes and walked into the bathroom.

"India?"

I stepped into the shower and stared at Ruben's soapy muscle rippled back and firm buttocks. He stepped under the water cascade but didn't turn around.

"India, you sure you ready for this?"

I laced my arms under his and held him to me. "I'm tired of contemplating. I'm going on pure feeling. Look at me." I turned him around and put my hand under his chin. "Look at me please."

His eyes traced my bare torso. He breathed deeply and I felt his manhood bump my leg. I wiped the suds from his forehead and stepped back so he could see all of me. We took each other in, mapping out one another's bodies with our eyes.

"You're stunning India, you know that."

"You not too bad yourself," I giggled and felt my face flush.

We made sweet love in the shower, the warm water rushing over our bound forms. He was unhurried with his every touch. He wrapped my legs around him and entered me with a gentleness that made me shiver.

"I've been dreaming about this for so long, India," he whispered in between open mouthed kisses to my neck and face. "You feel me, ma?"

"Yes, baby. Oh God, yes," I gasped.

I felt our bodies tense as we readied to burst. It felt amazing, much too remarkable to ask him to pull out. We came together, moaning into one another's mouths. He held me against the wall, still inside me, smoothed my wet hair from my face and put his forehead to mine.

"Damn, India *mía,* what are you doing to me?" He held my face firmly and kissed my eyelids. "Don't hurt me, India. Please don't hurt me. I couldn't handle it. I'm in love with you, India. Head over heels in love with you. Everything about you." I tasted salt when I kissed his face and knew he was crying.

"I won't. Trust me please. I ..."

"Don't say it 'cause I said it. Don't." He unwrapped my legs from his waist and washed me. We stepped out of the tub and he dried me off, leaving his dripping body exposed. I grabbed the towel and dried him off. I dabbed his face with a corner of the towel.

"I'd never hurt you babe. I ..."

"Ssshhh." He put his finger to my lips. "Your actions speak for you, India. I know."

He led me to the bed and lay me down, unwrapping the towel from around my body. He scanned my form and removed the towel under me. His thick, long penis was still rock hard. He lay down next to me and circled my stiff nipples with the tips of his fingers, moved down my abdomen and traced my belly button. "You're perfect. Just perfect. From head to toe, perfect."

He brought his mouth to my vagina and with the very tip of his tongue, edged along my clitoris, blowing warm air as he went along. I squirmed, cupping my breasts into my trembling hands. He ate me slowly, moving his tongue down the length of my pussy, down into my ass and back up. When he heard my groans grow louder and my breathing becoming heavy, he resurfaced. I whined in frustration.

"Not yet, India. I want you to come when I'm inside you. Ssshhh."

He tried to enter me but I quickly maneuvered my body from under him and flipped him over. He laughed. "Look at you."

"My turn."

I kissed his face and took his earlobe into my mouth, as I licked his neck, he pulled back. "Oooh, that's my weak spot, India. Be careful. You're gonna bring the tiger out of a nigga."

I giggled and moved down his body, lacing him with open

mouth kisses. I licked his head with the tip of my tongue and wrapped my hand around his penis, jerking him slowly. I saw him dig his fingernails into my duvet and bite his bottom lip. He took the pillow and propped his head up so he could watch me. I sniggered and began to suck him off. I took his length down my throat, careful to inhale so I wouldn't gag. I ran my tongue up and down his shaft and curled my lips around my teeth as I stroked him. He began to pant as my strokes became quicker and deeper. I felt his body squeeze and his veins throb in my mouth. I then removed him from my mouth and moved up towards his face.

"No, no, no. Not yet."

He laughed and flipped me over, using his weight and strength to pin me beneath him. "You little tease," he jested. He put his tongue deep into my mouth and entered me. He squeezed my ass and pushed himself deep inside me. I shrieked as I felt him wiggle around within. He stopped suddenly and pulled back.

"Ay India, did I hurt you? I'm ..."

"No," I panted. "Don't stop!" I pulled him back and pushed him into me. "Don't stop."

He pushed my body down onto him, slipping his hands under my arms and onto my shoulders. He pumped me steadily, biting my neck and listening to my wails of ecstasy. He fed off my reaction; he thrust into me slowly then went faster as I moaned louder and louder.

"You coming, baby? You coming? I feel you. Ay, India *mía*,

I feel you," he whispered as I gushed all over him. He pushed his length into me and tears streamed down into my hair as I felt his dick pulsate and spray my insides.

He fell onto me, exhausted and sweating. I rubbed my hands up his back. "I love you, Ruben." I held him to my breast as our combined fluids oozed out of me and dripped down my ass.

"We should really go wash up, India."

I lay there dog-tired. "No puedo," I whined. "I'm sooo tired."

He rose, scooped me up and plopped me into the bathtub. "Wash that ass," he laughed. He stepped into the tub next to me and we washed each other. I stayed in the shower, letting the water spill over me after he got out. When I walked into the room, I froze at the picture on the TV screen. Fabian's mug shot taunted me. Ruben saw the look of dread on my face and knew.

"That's him, isn't it?" he asked, anger rising in his throat.

I sat on the bed. "What did they say? What's going on?"

Ruben bit his lip. "Well" he breathed deeply readying himself. "A jailhouse snitch has implicated him in the shooting of a Carlos Peña. From the look on your face, I can see you know about that. Fabian's lawyer went public and said that his client is innocent of these charges. He also said ..." Ruben looked at me, his brow creased with worry. "India, he's never gonna hurt you again. I'd never let him hurt you."

"Tell me, Ruben," I said firmly. "Tell me!" I violently wiped the tears from my face, furious that Fabian could still incite such fear in me.

"His lawyer said that he's making a motion to have all charges dropped. He claims the police searched his apartment without a warrant and there's insufficient evidence to tie him to the kidnapping and rape."

I fell onto the bed, heaving. Ruben grabbed my shaking form and rocked me. "Don't worry, Indiecita. The DA said they have a strong case against him. That they have DNA evidence and fingerprints tying him to the crime. That the warrant was unnecessary because they had sufficient cause to search his crib. Don't worry, India. Please ..."

I pulled away from him abruptly. "What do you mean don't worry. How am I not supposed to worry? You don't know what he's capable of! He'll kill me! He'll come find me and kill me and everyone I love! Don't you see! It's not over! He swore it wasn't over and he was right! It's not! He won't rest until I'm dead!"

"Relax, India. I'm here! I won't let him do anything to you!"

"And what the fuck are you going to do? Huh? Tell me?" I was so angry I lashed out at Ruben because he was the closest one to me.

"So that's how you see me? I'm some fuckin' punk nigga that can't do shit to protect you from this beast? I see. Thanks for believing

in me!" He got up and grabbed his clothes. I stared at him, sobbing as he dressed. "I'm not a fuckin' *cobarde*, India. You see me all corporate, a suit and tie nigga and you think I'm a pussy? Damn ma! I told you, I fuckin' love you! *¡Te adoro!* I love you like I've never loved anybody in my life! If I have to die or go to jail to protect you, I will!" He stormed towards the door.

"No! Don't leave! Please don't leave me! I need you Ruben, please!" I collapsed at his feet. "I'm sorry. I'm just scared. I can't go through this again! I can't take this! Oh God!"

Ruben kneeled down and took me into his arms. This was our first argument, our first disagreement. I was mortified that it was because of Fabian.

"India, I'm gonna take care of it. I'll make sure he'll never hurt you. Let me do this."

I saw a look of rage in Ruben's eyes that frightened me. "What are you gonna do? Ruben please, just leave it to the courts. Let it be."

"The courts won't protect you, India. I'm the only one who can. I know what to do, who to call."

"No! I can't let you get involved in this. Please! Promise me you won't do anything crazy! *¡Prométeme!*" I brought his face to mine. "*¡Prométeme!*"

He sighed deeply and put his face in my neck. "*Te prometo...* for now but if this nigga even dares to contact you or threaten you in any way, it's over for him. You hear me? I'm not playing, India."

"Okay. Just please, stay with me tonight." He played with my hair until I fell asleep. The following morning when I awoke, he was gone.

45

"Hi, India *mía*. How are you?"

"I'm okay. I just got a call from the prosecutor. The trial is in a month. They expect me to testify. I'm scared, pa."

"Don't be. I'll be there with you. I told you, he's out of your life for good. You just have to do this to put him away then it's over."

"Where'd you go this morning?"

"I, um ..."

"Please don't lie to me, Ruben. *No me mientas.*" The silence on the line went on for far too long. My heart lashed my chest cavity. "Ruben, what did you do? I asked you not to..."

"I didn't do anything. I just made some calls, that's it. Put some people on alert just in case. Look, I told you I'd be honest with you. I have a lot to tell you, India. There's some stuff you don't know about me. I put it behind me but … Look, I'm on my way right now. I'll be there in twenty. *Besos*."

I held the phone to my ear long after Ruben has hung up. I wondered what Ruben was about to confess to me. I breathed heavily, trying to knead away the knot that had developed in my stomach.

When Ruben arrived, his shoulders were slumped over. He looked stressed and hesitated before meeting my eyes.

"What's wrong, babe? What's going on?"

"India, sit down. Just listen. Don't talk, just listen." Ruben sat next to me and put his hands on mine. "I never lied to you and never will. That's why I'm telling you this. There's just some things I didn't tell you about me because I was worried about how you'd react. After hearing everything you'd gone through with Fabian, I thought that if I told you, you'd disappear from my life. I didn't want to lose you, India. I don't want to lose you now and I hope you won't leave me after I tell you this." He heaved a sigh and began.

"Years ago, I was a drug dealer. I worked the streets around 163rd with my older brother. I was small time, nothing big, just making enough money to live and floss a little. My brother got greedy. He got in contact with this dealer he'd gone to school with and started doing some crazy shit, moving big weight. I told him not to do it, told him he was crazy, that it wasn't worth it. He didn't listen. He was so fuckin' stupid!" He shook his head and buried his face in his hands. I put my hand on his head but he pulled away. "One day this nigga shows up with like 20 keys, says his boy gave it to him to move. I was suspicious but he promised me there was nothin' dirty going on so I believed him. He was my brother, *¿entiendes?* So I helped him move it. We made some good money, too good. I started hearing on the streets that my brother had knocked somebody for the drugs. I tried to talk to him about it but he wouldn't listen." Ruben looked at me, his face was contorted with agony. "My brother is Carlos Peña, India. He stole those drugs from Fabian."

I pulled away from him horrified. "What?"

"India, please!" He grabbed my wrists and forcefully kept me seated next to him. "I didn't know. I swear I didn't know. I didn't put the pieces together until I heard the news yesterday. When my brother spoke of Fabian, he called him Fabe. I didn't know they were the same people. I never met him myself. India, please believe me. Please!"

I cringed as he squeezed my wrists tighter. "Ruben, you're hurting me. Please ..."

He let me go suddenly realizing how hard he was grabbing me. "I'm sorry. I... That nigga left my brother handicapped. He couldn't move his legs, couldn't have kids." Ruben teared uncontrollably. I wanted to soothe him but I couldn't. I was still digesting this new information.

"Carlos always suspected Fabian but he just couldn't prove it." He looked at me with bloodshot eyes. "He killed himself two years ago. He couldn't live like that – unable to walk, dependent on other people. I found him. He overdosed." He crumpled to the couch shaking violently.

"Ay baby. Why didn't you tell me? Oh God."

"I'm sorry, India. Sorry I didn't tell you. I couldn't. I didn't know how. I haven't been able to talk about that since it happened. Then yesterday when I saw the news it all came back. I made the connections and... That motherfucker destroyed my life, my family! My mother died months after my brother. His suicide killed her. I was left alone. Everybody I loved is gone ..." He began crying loudly releasing a misery he'd held within for years. "Don't leave me, India. I got no one. I'm alone except for you. You're the first person I've let in since everything happened. I ..."

"I'm not goin' anywhere, Ruben. We're in this together, okay?" He whimpered into my breast until he fell asleep.

Ruben tossed and turned in his sleep. He was plagued with nightmares for the next few nights. When I questioned him, he admitted to talking to some old school dealer friends he knew from his street days. They considered his brother their brother as well. When he interrogated them about Fabian, they all said they knew him from the game. They'd heard about the allegations of Fabian's involvement in Carlos's attempted murder and weren't surprised. Rumors had been circulating about his involvement for years.

"Fabian was known in the streets for being a loose canon. People did business with him but kept him at arm's length 'cause they knew what a sheisty nigga he was. The more I hear about him, the more I wonder how you could have gotten mixed up with such a trife nigga."

"I wasn't from the streets, baby. I didn't know any better. Fabian showed me a different face than he showed the world … well he did at first."

"Well, that nigga's never gonna hurt you again. Not as long as I'm breathing." I looked at Ruben with arched eyebrows. "No, don't worry I didn't put a hit out on him or anything. Honestly, I don't have to. From what I hear, there's a lot of people out to get him. He's lucky he's in solitary confinement 'cause he might be dead by now. That nigga has a lot of enemies."

"That doesn't surprise me. Anyway, I have a meeting with the D.A. in a couple of days. They want to prepare me for my testimony. I don't want to but I have to. The D.A. says I'm their strongest witness. You know that nigga is now trying to say those drugs were mine?"

Ruben jumped up. "What?!"

"Yeah." I laughed. "How pathetic is that. I'm not worried. They have months of surveillance on him. There's no evidence to implicate me. His fingerprints were all over the bags of drugs, mine weren't."

"You ready to testify?"

"No but I don't have a choice. I have to confront him, tell my story. He has to pay for what he did to me. It's the only way."

"I'll be there for you the entire time."

"I wanted to talk to you about that." I'd been mulling over this since the prosecutor called me. Although I needed Ruben there, I felt more comfortable if he wasn't. I was afraid that if Fabian saw Ruben, he'd go after him too. "I don't think you should go."

"Excuse me? Are you kidding?"

"No, I'm not. Babe, if he sees you with me..."

"If he sees me, what? What's he gonna do? If he wants to bring it, let him bring it. You're my lady now and he's gonna have to live with that. I'm going, India, and that's final."

Although I was nervous, it comforted me that Ruben insisted on going. I knew his presence would give me strength. I kissed him. "Okay, okay. I just couldn't live with myself if anything happened to you, babe. I love you too much."

"Don't worry about me. I got this. My job is to protect you not the opposite, okay?"

That night we made love on every surface of my apartment. A couple of days later, as I readied myself for my appointment with the DA, Ruben watched me from the bed as I dressed.

"India, can I ask you something?"

"Go ahead, baby. What's on your mind?"

"Are you on birth control?"

I stopped pulling my jeans up mid-thigh. "Kinda late for that question."

"I know. We just haven't been exactly careful, you know."

"Yeah," I sighed. I'd tried not to think about how careless we were being. Ruben loved coming inside of me and it felt so good, I never protested. "No, I'm not."

Ruben nodded his head pensively. "Have you put any thought into what we'd do if you got pregnant?"

"What we'd do?"

"Yeah we. We're in this together, remember?"

I walked over and sat next to him on the bed. "No, I haven't put any thought into it, baby. We have been careless and we should start thinking about some birth control options. I guess we've been so caught up in the moment, we haven't given it a second thought."

"Well, we should. I love you and I'm here but I don't think either of us is ready for a baby."

"I'm certainly not."

"But if it happened, I wouldn't want you to take it out." I rose from the bed quickly. I wasn't ready to have this discussion with him. He pulled me back. "India *mía*, don't avoid the issue. I wouldn't want you to abort our baby. Everything happens for a reason, right?"

I kissed his forehead. "Well, hopefully we won't have to worry about that, right." I finished dressing and we sped out the door together.

46

The next few weeks passed by in a blur. The frigid morning of the trial, I awoke nauseous and feeling feverish. I attributed it to anxiety about the case. The last time I'd seen Fabian's detestable face, he'd abducted and assaulted me in the most insidious manner. It was only natural that I'd be squeamish.

When I entered the courtroom, I locked eyes with Fabian's mother. She looked gaunt and worn. I pitied her despite her apparent loathing of me. Ruben protectively grabbed my hand and led me to a middle row, far from Maria's derisive glare. When Fabian was brought in, I clutched Ruben's hand tightly. My heart raced when he looked at me and grinned sinisterly. His face dropped when he saw

Ruben holding me.

In his opening statement, the DA revealed that Fabian was being charged with an extensive list of charges including kidnapping, rape, sexual assault, battery, possession of narcotics, and drug trafficking. Although charges were likely to be brought against him for the attempted murder of the now deceased Carlos Peña, he would have to face those charges in a separate trial.

I was the first witness to be called forth. My knees knocked as I walked to the stand and purposely evaded Fabian's glare.

"Can you please state your name and relation to the defendant."

"My name is India Maldonado and I am Fabian's ex-girlfriend." The DA had me describe myself to demonstrate my character for the jury. "Well, I'm a recent graduate of Columbia University and am currently pursuing a career in writing."

"Columbia, the Ivy League University?"

"Yes, that's the one."

"How did you meet the defendant, Ms. Maldonado?" I explained my first encounter with Fabian and how he'd lured me into his snare. The prosecutor painted me out to be a victim from the beginning. He had me go into how I'd tried to flee from Fabian, omitting of course how I'd set him up and stolen his money.

"Now we're going to discuss the events that led up to this trial. What occurred on the night in question?"

"Well, I'd spent the day rollerblading. I was on my way back to the dorm when I was pulled into a car. When I came to, I was tied up on a bed." I exhaled noisily and looked at Ruben.

He gave me a thumbs up and mouthed, "You're doing fine."

"Can you describe the room?" I closed my eyes and pictured my prison in my head. I described it for the jury. Though I was still feeling somewhat sick, I surprised myself at how composed I'd been thus far. That changed at the sight of the picture of my prison.

"I'd like to submit Exhibit A as evidence." My stomach turned and I winced at the acrid taste that filled my mouth.

"Now I'm going to have to ask you about the events that ensued. Take your time, Ms. Maldonado."

As I disclosed the torture and sexual assault that followed, my shoulders shook. I couldn't control the wave of emotion. Tears ran down Ruben's face as I spoke. Then I looked at Fabian and the look of contempt on his face reenergized me. I wiped my face, drank some water the judge offered and relayed the tale of Fabian's attack. I glowered at him as I spoke; I had to show him that I wasn't going to let him frighten me into submission. When I was done, I looked at the jury and noticed that several of the jurors dabbed their eyes. The judge then adjourned the trial for lunch.

I couldn't eat anything. I knew that I had to go back on the stand and the thought destroyed my appetite. My stomach still hadn't settled completely. As we walked back to the court, I suddenly felt a rush of bile in my throat. I leaned over and threw up.

"Indiecita, you okay?" Ruben held my hair while I vomited.

"Yeah, it's just *nervios*. I'll be fine."

The rest of my testimony consisted of questions about Fabian's dealings. Unfortunately, Fabian didn't really keep me in the know about his transactions so there was little information I could provide but the prosecutor assured me that what I had imparted was sufficient. The defense lawyer struggled in his cross examination of me. While he tried to portray me as a bitter ex, he failed miserably.

"Aren't you doing this just to get back at him for leaving you?"

I laughed heartily. "I would have been glad if he'd left me. That's what I wanted - to be left alone. Fabian couldn't deal with that."

"Ms. Maldonado, you make yourself out to be an innocent party but you resided in the residence where the drugs were found. How could possibly you have been unaware of his dealings?"

"Look, I've never denied knowing that he was a drug dealer. I was young and stupid and in love. But I was never directly involved in his business. He kept that separate and apart or so I thought. I trusted him when he said that he'd never put me in danger. I didn't know about the drugs in the apartment until the police informed me of them." I remembered finding the kilos and the feeling of dread they stirred in me. What if I had been in the apartment when it was raided? That would have destroyed my life. I felt a surge of hatred at the thought of him putting me in that predicament.

"That sounds highly unlikely, Ms. Maldonado."

"It may sound it but that's the truth. My fingerprints weren't found on the bags were they? His were. That's evidence enough."

"No, that simply means you didn't touch the bags, it doesn't mean you weren't witness to it." He walked away and with a sneer said he was done questioning me.

As I walked off the witness stand, Fabian smiled at me evilly. "Hello, India. How ya been?"

Before I could say anything the judge spoke. "Mr. Holloway, if you can't control your client, I'll have him removed from my courtroom. I won't stand for any nonsense."

"I didn't ..." Fabian began to defend himself

"Ssssshhh!" Mr. Holloway hushed Fabian quickly and whispered sternly in his ear. I held my head up and walked to my seat next to Ruben.

The trial lasted another six agonizing days. My heart stopped when the DA called Lynette Cintrón to the stand. I stared open mouthed as she walked through the doors and up to the stand. She avoided Fabian's fierce look.

She proceeded to describe her relationship with Fabian, admitting to having been his mistress for years and having been witness to his many drug transactions. She then explained how she'd helped him stalk me from the inside. She sobbed as she told of how he'd manipulated her into helping him.

The prosecutor's cross examination was brutal. He made her out to be a liar and jilted lover. She stuttered in response to his interrogations and fell apart on the stand. I pitied her because despite her betrayal, she didn't deserve this. When she walked off the stand, our eyes met. She mouthed, "I'm so sorry" and sped out of the courtroom.

I wasn't surprised to find that the defense had opted not to let Fabian testify. He remained expressionless for the remainder of the trial, avoiding Ruben's fierce glare.

The most comical part of the case occurred when Fabian's mother took the stand as a character witness on the part of defense. She painted her son out as a "good boy" who fell victim to the wiles of whorish women including myself. I scoffed when she claimed that her son was not a man of the streets. She argued that he worked in her brother's store but upon being cross examined by the DA couldn't explain why he wasn't on the payroll or the fact that there was no record of him ever having filed taxes.

The jurors took a surprisingly long three days to deliberate on the case and charges. When they reentered the court room, Fabian stood pokerfaced as they read their decision. To my glee, he was found guilty on all charges.

I collapsed into Ruben's arms as I heard Fabian's mother screaming in the background. She came at me, swearing in her thick Spanish accent, but was stopped by the guards.

" *¡Máldita sucia!* Dis is all your fault! You did dis to my son!"

Ruben stood in front of me and glowered at her. "Back up, lady," he warned.

" ¡Eso es un cuero, niño! ¡Ten mucho cuidao con esa!" she ranted.

He laughed at her, took my hand, kissed it and led me out of the courtroom. Two weeks later Fabian was scheduled to learn his fate.

I became increasingly sick as the sentencing day approached. I continued to blame it on jittery nerves but Ruben wasn't buying it. One day he came home with a pregnancy test.

"What the hell is that for? You pregnant, babe?" I half joked. The prospect of being with child scared me shitless.

"Let's just make sure, India."

I urinated in the cup and stood over it with him as the test stick marinated in it. When the plus sign appeared, Ruben jumped. He embraced me and screamed, "Oh my God, I'm going to be a father!"

I stood there unable to say or feel anything. Just the night before, we'd celebrated with my Mom and Professor Daines my finishing the first draft of my memoir and Fabian's conviction. I couldn't believe what was happening now.

I sat on the edge of the tub and stared at my feet. The tiles seemed to mock me.

"India, you okay?"

"I don't know how to feel babe. I ..." Then the tears came

and didn't relent for what seemed like hours. "How can I be a mom? I'm not ready for this. I'm still getting over the horror that's been my life and I'm expected to bring another life into this world? I can't... I can't..."

Ruben held me while I purged. "You can and you will. It's just what the cosmos have in store for you." He lifted my face to his. "You're ready for this, Indiecita. Your life culminates to this. Everything you've experienced, the joy and the pain, culminates to this task, the central, most crucial duty of your existence. You're going to be an amazing mother because of it not in spite of it. Have faith, India."

I rubbed my belly and wept. I knew I couldn't abort my child. Not because Ruben wouldn't allow it but because I couldn't allow it. This was the hand that I was dealt and I would have to come to grips with it.

Morning sickness incapacitated me for the next few days. On the day of the sentencing, I could barely dress myself I was so weak. Despite this, the idea of motherhood was slowly but surely losing it's fear-provoking effect. Yes, I was young and yes, my relationship was new, but I was thrilled by the image of my legacy being left on this earth long after I was gone. Somehow, my instincts told me that the child I was carrying was female and nothing and no one could tell me otherwise. Ruben insisted that I should prepare myself mentally for either but I wouldn't have it. I trusted what my heart told me.

I accepted that motherhood was going to be difficult, more arduous than anything I'd experienced, but it was worth it because it was for my seed, a life I would shape and mold into a strong being with conviction and integrity. I'd work to establish a solid friendship with her so that she'd come to me when she needed guidance rather seek advice from another who would lead her astray. I understood that I couldn't possibly be there 24/7, but I vowed to provide her with the proper ethics so that when it was time for her to make those life-altering decisions, she'd hear my voice in her ear telling her not to be a follower, that she was the master of her destiny. I promised myself that I'd be honest with my child, tell her of my mistakes. When she was old enough I intended on confiding the misery I'd endured at the hands of Fabian. I hoped she'd learn from my errors in judgment.

When we entered the courtroom, I eyed Fabian pensively. I silently thanked the Higher Power that I'd never had a child with that man. I couldn't fathom what type of father he would be, certainly abusive and sadistic. When he looked back in my direction, I unconsciously put my hands over my stomach.

The judge asked if anyone wanted to speak before he announced the sentence. Despite my frailty, I felt compelled to say some last words to Fabian. I walked to the podium and leaned on it for support. I looked into Fabian's dark eyes.

"You deserve the worst because that's what you've given

everyone who's crossed your path. I hate you for stealing my innocence but pity you for not realizing the extent of your immorality. It's over now, Fabian. You can't hurt me anymore. You can't control me or manipulate me. Now you can sit in your jail cell and dream about the life I'm living on the outside while you rot on the inside. Enjoy it!"

I walked away defiantly and buried my face in Ruben's chest when the judge hit him with the maximum sentence, fifty years with no chance of parole for 30. "Your crimes were heinous but it's your lack of remorse that I find most appalling."

As he was led away, Fabian stared at me with anger and revulsion. "It ain't over!" he bellowed. A ferocious maternal instinct overwhelmed me. The first thing that crossed my mind was my baby, protecting her from this devil incarnate.

Out of nowhere, Ruben stepped in front of me and stared Fabian down. "It is over, *hijo de puta*! You so much as write her a letter and you'll regret the day you were born. I dare you, motherfucker! Bring it!" he yelled as Fabian was pulled out the door, a look of sick pleasure on his face.

Ruben turned to me and led me out of the courtroom. When we stepped outside, he wrapped his arms around me and crooned, "It's finished, India. He can never hurt you again. Now we can direct our attention to what's really important." He rubbed my stomach with paternal affection. "Are my nenas hungry?"

"Nenas? I thought you said I should prepare myself for a

boy?" I joked with a flutter of my lashes.

"You say it's a girl, I believe you. She's growing inside of you, not me. You'd know better than I would."

"So, you admit to being wrong? My God, a man exists that can admit to being wrong."

"I have and I can." He smirked. "So, are my nenas hungry?"

"A little. I still feel sick though."

"You'll probably be feeling like that for a while or at least that's what the book says."

"What book?" I asked perplexed. He pulled out What to Expect When You're Expecting. "When did you get that?"

"I bought it a couple of weeks ago after we talked about how not careful we were being. I bought it just in case and well, I guess my intuition was right." He chuckled and rubbed my belly.

I beamed. Now that Fabian was imprisoned, I could carry on with my life without looking over my shoulder. My life was starting anew and the path ahead looked rosy. I was finally free to enjoy my pregnancy. I had a good man by my side that adored me and would die to protect me and our child. I'd just finished my memoir and was eager to pursue a career in writing. At long last the cosmos were endowing me with happiness and joy to make up for my extended ordeal.

I looked up at the sky and raised my hands high above my head. "Thank you God! Thank you!" I looked at Ruben and giggled.

"Let's get some food, pa. I think I can eat and keep it down."

"Let's go to Carmine's."

When we walked into the restaurant, I was surprised to see my mom and Professor Daines sitting at a table. They alleged that they'd met up for lunch and that our meeting them was entirely coincidental but I wasn't convinced. I looked at Ruben as we sat down and ordered drinks and appetizers. They were elated to hear of Fabian's sentencing. We celebrated with a toast. My mom wrinkled her brow at me when I ordered apple juice instead of wine.

I looked at my mom. She looked so content and proud, so at peace. I realized this was the perfect time to tell her that she would soon be a grandmother.

"I have some news," I started.

"Before you do that I have some news," Joanna interrupted. "I think I found a publisher. Remember that friend I told you about, the one that works at Simon and Schuster? Well, I sent him a couple of stories from your memoirs and he absolutely raved about them. I've set up a meeting in two weeks." She squeezed my hand with excitement.

My mom smiled wide. "*¡Viste!* I told you that all good things come in time. Look, now you have *un buen hombre* in your life and you have your book to look forward to." She leaned over and kissed my

cheek. She'd met Ruben three weeks into our relationship and fell in love with him instantly. When she saw how tender and attentive he was, she told me that he was the one I was meant to be with. Initially, I was abashed by her honesty, after all our relationship was so new, but now I saw that she'd been right all along.

Ruben looked around the table and smiled at us. "Well, we have big news too but first thing's first." He stood up from the table and got on one knee.

My jaw dropped. I couldn't believe he was about to propose. I tried to stop him but he wouldn't listen.

"India, mi India linda, you are the best thing that's ever happened to me. You are my earth, my everything. Let me be your sun. Let me take care of you and love you forever. Marry me, Indiecita. Marry me." The entire restaurant erupted in applause.

"You don't have to do this, baby. You don't have to propose because ..." I stopped and looked at my mom and Joanna.

"Ma, I'm pregnant and I think Ruben is proposing because he feels obligated." I turned to Ruben. "I'll be with you regardless. You don't have to feel forced to marry me. I know you'll be there for me and the baby."

My mom looked from me to Ruben and back to me. "Ruben, did you know this when we went to pick out the ring?" she demanded.

"No. I'm doing this because I want to spend my life with your daughter."

"You went to... When?" I stuttered.

"Yes, I got the ring before I found out about the baby. I want to marry you, pregnant or not."

I threw my arms around him and screamed, "Yes, I'll marry you! Yes!"

AFTERWORD

Despite Ruben's objections, I refused to marry him before the birth of our child. I wouldn't even set a date. There was no doubt in my mind that I wanted to marry this man but I wanted to focus on enjoying our pregnancy and one another.

I was hugely creative while I was with child. In six months, I compiled a book of short stories and vignettes, wrote a book of poetry and started a novel. My memoir was published when I was eight and a half months pregnant. I went into labor at my book release party. There was no better way to celebrate my officially becoming an author.

Solae Maldonado Sanchez came into the world after twenty excruciating hours of labor. She was a healthy 8 lbs 5 oz. Ruben held my hand the entire time and bawled like a baby when he saw our child come into the world.

When Solae was placed in my arms, I counted her fingers and toes and cradled her to my breast. "Life is hard," I whispered. "It hurts but it's moments like this that make it worth the while."

Augustus Publishing was created to unify minds with entertaining, hard-hitting tales from a hood near you. Hip Hop literature interprets contemporary times and connects to readers through shared language, culture and artistic expression. From street tales and erotica to coming-of age sagas, our stories are endearing, filled with drama, imagination and laced with a Hip Hop steez.

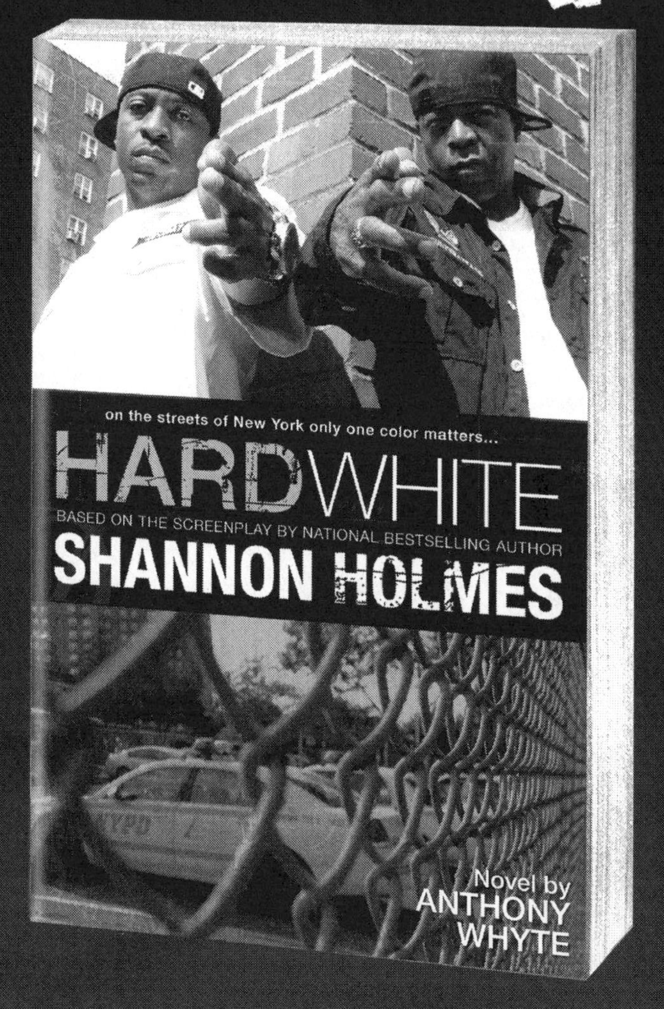

Hard White: On the street of New York only on color matters
Novel By Anthony Whyte Based on the screenplay by Shannon Holmes

The streets are pitch black...A different shade of darkness has drifted to the North Bronx neighborhood known as Edenwald. Sleepless nights, there is no escaping dishonesty, disrespect, suspicion, ignorance, hostility, treachery, violence, karma... Hard White metered out to the residents. Two, Melquan and Precious have big dreams but must overcome much in order to manifest theirs. Hard White the novel is a story of triumph and tribulations of two people's journey to make it despite the odds. Nail biting drama you won't ever forget...Once you pick it up you can't put it down. Deftly written by Anthony Whyte based on the screenplay by Shannon Holmes, the story comes at you fast, furiously offering an insight to what it takes to get off the streets. It shows a woman's unWlimited love for her man. Precious is a rider and will do it all again for her man, Melquan... His love for the street must be bloodily severed. Her love for him will melt the coldest heart...Together their lives hang precariously over the crucible of Hard White. Read the novel and see why they make the perfect couple.

$14.95 / / 9780982541531

When Love Turns To Hate
By Sharron Doylee

Petie is back regulating from down south. He rides with a new ruthless partner, and they're all about making fast money. The partners mercilessly go after a shady associate who is caught in an FBI sting and threatens their road to riches. Petie and his two sons have grown apart. Renee, their mother, has to make a big decision when one of her sons wild-out. Desperately, she tries to keep her world from crumbling while holding onto what's left of her family. Venus fights for life after suffering a brutal physical attack. Share goes to great lengths to make sure her best friend's attacker stays ruined forever. Crazy entertaining and teeming with betrayal, corruption, and murder, When Love Turns To Hate is mixed with romance gone awry. The drama will leave you panting for more....

$14.95 / / 9780982541517

Street Chic
By Anthony Whyte

A new case comes across the desk of detective Sheryl Street, from the Dade county larceny squad in Miami. Pursuing the investigation she discovers that it threatens to unfold some details of her life she thought was left buried in the Washington Heights area of New York City. Her duties as detective pits her against a family that had emotionally destabilized her. Street ran away from a world she wanted nothing to do with. The murder of a friend brings her back as law and order. Surely as night time follows daylight, Street's forced into a resolve she cannot walk away from. Loyalty is tested when a deadly choice has to be made. When you read this dark and twisted novel you'll find out if allegiance to her family wins Street over. A most interesting moral conundrum exists in the dramatic tension that is Street Chic.

$14.95 / / 9780982541500

SMUT central
By Brandon McCalla

Markus Johnson, so mysterious he barely knows who he is. An infant left at the doorstep of an orphanage. After fleeing his refuge, he was taken in by a couple with a perverse appetite for sexual indiscretions, only to become a star in the porn industry... Dr. Nancy Adler, a shrink who gained a peculiar patient, unlike any she has ever encountered. A young African American man who faints upon sight of a woman he has never met, having flashbacks of a past he never knew existed. A past that contradicts the few things he knows about himself... Sex and lust tangled in a web so disgustingly tantalizing and demented. Something evil, something demonic... Something beyond the far reaches of a porn stars mind, peculiar to a well established shrink, leaving an old NYPD detective on the verge of solving a case that has been a dead end for years... all triggered by desires for a mysterious woman...

$14.95 / / 9780982541586

Dead And Stinkin'
By Stephen Hewett

A collection of three deadly novellas, Dead and Stinkin' invokes the themes of Jamaican folklore and traditions West Indian storytelling in a modern setting.

$14.95 / / 9780982541555

Power of the P
By James Hendricks

Erotica at its gritty best, Power of the P is the seductive story of an entrepreneur who wields his powerful status in unimaginable — and sometimes unethical — ways. This exotic ride through the underworld of sex and prostitution in the hood explores how sex is leveraged to gain advantage over friends and rivals alike, and how sometimes the white collar world and the streets aren't as different as we thought they were.

$14.95 / / 9780982541579

America's Soul
By Erick S Gray

Soul has just finished his 18-month sentence for a parole violation. Still in love with his son's mother, America, he wants nothing more than for them to become a family and move on from his past. But while Soul was in prison, America's music career started blowing up and she became entangled in a rocky relationship with a new man, Kendall. Kendall is determined to keep his woman by his side, and America finds herself caught in a tug of war between the two men. Soul turns his attention to battling the street life that landed him in jail — setting up a drug program to rid the community of its tortuous meth problem — but will Soul's efforts cross his former best friend, the murderous drug kingpin Omega?

$14.95 / / 9780982541548

GHETTO GIRLS IV

Young Luv

ESSENCE BESTSELLING AUTHOR
ANTHONY WHYTE

Ghetto Girls IV Young Luv
$14.95 // 9780979281662

Ghetto Girls
$14.95 // 0975945319

Ghetto Girls Too
$14.95 // 0975945300

Ghetto Girls 3 Soo Hood
$14.95 // 0975945351

THE BEST OF THE STREET CHRONICLES TODAY, THE **GHETTO GIRLS SERIES** IS A WONDERFULLY HYPNOTIC ADVENTURE THAT DELVES INTO THE CONVOLUTED MINDS OF CRIMINALS AND THE DARK WORLD OF POLICE CORRUPTION. YET, THERE IS SOMETHING THRILLING AND SURPRISINGLY TENDER ABOUT THIS ONGOING YOUNG-ADULT SAGA FILLED WITH MAD FLAVA.

Love and a Gangsta

author // **ERICK S GRAY**

This explosive sequel to **Crave All Lose All**. Soul and America were together ten years 'til Soul's incarceration for drugs. Faithfully, she waited four years for his return. Once home they find life ain't so easy anymore. America believes in holding her man down and expects Soul to be as committed. His lust for fast money rears its ugly head at the same time America's music career takes off. From shootouts, to hustling and thugging life, Soul and his man, Omega, have done it. Omega is on the come-up in the drug-game of South Jamaica, Queens. Using ties to a Mexican drug cartel, Omega has Queens in his grip. His older brother, Rahmel, was Soul's cellmate in an upstate prison. Rahmel, a man of God, tries to counsel Soul. Omega introduces New York to crystal meth. Misery loves company and on the road to the riches and spoils of the game, Omega wants the only man he can trust, Soul, with him. Love between Soul and America is tested by an unforgivable greed that leads quickly to deception and murder.

$14.95 // 9780979281648

The lights went out and the mayhem began.

It's gritty in the city but hotter in Brooklyn where a small community in east Flatbush must come to grips with its greatest threat, self-destruction. August 14 and 15, 2003, the eastern section of the United States is crippled by a major shortage of electrical power, the worst in US history. Blackout, the spellbinding novel is based on the epic motion picture, directed by Jerry Lamothe. A thoroughly riveting story with delectable details of families caught in a harsh 48 hours of random violent acts, exploding in deadly conflict. There's a message in everything… even the bullet. The author vividly places characters on the stage of life and like pieces on a chess-board, expertly moves them to a tumultuous end. Voila! Checkmate, a literary triumph. Blackout is a masterpiece. This heart-stopping, page-turning drama is moving fast. Blackout is destined to become an American classic.

BASED ON SCREENPLAY BY **JERRY LaMOTHE**

Inspired by true events

US $14.95 CAN $20.95
ISBN 978-0-9820653-0-3

CASWELL COMMUNICATIONS

A POWERFUL UNFORGIVING STORY

CREATED BY HIP HOP LITERATURE'S BESTSELLING AUTHORS

THIS THREE-VOLUME KILLER STORY FEATURING FOREWORDS FROM
SHANNON HOLMES, K'WAN & **TREASURE BLUE**

Streets of New York vol. 1
$14.95 // 9780979281679

Streets of New York vol. 2
$14.95 // 9780979281662

Streets of New York vol. 3
$14.95 // 9780979281662

AN EXCITING, ENCHANTING... A FUNNY, THRILLING AND EXHILARATING RIDE THROUGH THE ROUGH NEIGHBORHOODS OF THE GRITTY CITY. THE MOST FUN YOU CAN LEGALLY HAVE WITHOUT ACTUALLY LIVING ON THE STREETS OF NEW YORK. READ THE STORY FROM HIP HOP LITERATURE TOP AUTHORS:

ERICK S. GRAY, MARK ANTHONY & **ANTHONY WHYTE**

Lipstick Diaries Part 2

A Provocative Look into the Female Perspective
Foreword by **WAHIDA CLARK**

Lipstick Diaries II is the second coming together of some of the most unique, talented female writers of Hip Hop Literature. Featuring a feast of short stories from today's top authors. **Genieva Borne, Camo, Endy, Brooke Green, Kineisha Gayle, the queen of hip hop lit; Carolyn McGill, Vanessa Martir, Princess Madison, Keisha Seignious**, and a blistering foreword served up by the queen of thug love; Ms. **Wahida Clark**. Lipstick Diaries II pulls no punches, there are no bars hold leaves no metaphor unturned. The anthology delivers a knockout with stories of pain and passion, love and virtue, profit and gain, ... all told with flair from the women's perspective. Lipstick Diaries II is a must-read for all.

$14.95 // 9780979281655

ENJOY THE MOST EXHILARATING RIDE THROUGH HIP HOP LITERATURE

CHECK OUT THESE PREVIOUS RELEASES FROM AUGUSTUS PUBLISHING

Lipstick Diaries
author // **VARIOUS AUTHORS**
$14.95 // 0975945394

A Boogie Down Story
author // **KEISHA SEIGNIOUS**
$14.95 // 0979281601

Crave All Lose All
author // **ERICK S GRAY**
$14.95 // 097928161X

If It Ain't One Thing It's Another
author // **SHARRON DOYLE**
$14.95 // 097594536X

Woman's Cry
author // **VANESSA MARTIR**
$14.95 // 0975945386

Booty Call *69
author // **ERICK S GRAY**
$14.95 // 0975945343

A Good Day To Die
author // **JAMES HENDRICKS**
$14.95 // 0975945327

Spot Rushers
author // **BRANDON McCALLA**
$14.95 // 0979281628

It Can Happen In a Minute
author // **S.M. JOHNSON**
$14.95 // 0975945378

Hustle Hard
author // **BLAINE MARTIN**
$14.95 // 0979281636

ORDER INFO

Mail us a list of the titles you would like and **$14.95** per Title + shipping charges **$3.95** for one book & **$1.00** for each additional book.
Make all checks payable to:
Augustus Publishing 33 Indian Rd. NY, NY 10034
Email: info@augustuspublishing.com

Bookstores & Distributors contact:
Publishers Group West | www.pgw.com
Customer Service 800-788-3123
1700 Fourth Street Berkeley, California 94710

AugustusPublishing.com